Boy Trouble at Trebizon

ANNE DIGBY

Boy Trouble at Trebizon

Illustrated by Gavin Rowe

A DRAGON BOOK

GRANADA
London Toronto Sydney New York

Published by Granada Publishing Limited in 1981
Reprinted in 1981, 1983

ISBN 0 583 30430 3

First published in Great Britain by
Granada Publishing Limited
Copyright © Anne Digby 1980

Granada Publishing Limited
Frogmore, St Albans, Herts AL2 2NF
and
36 Golden Square, London W1R 4AH
515 Madison Avenue, New York, NY 10022, USA
117 York Street, Sydney NSW 2000, Australia
100 Skyway Avenue, Rexdale, Ontario, M9W 3A6, Canada
61 Beach Road, Auckland, New Zealand

Made and printed in Great Britain by
Richard Clay (The Chaucer Press) Ltd,
Bungay, Suffolk
Set in Linotype Plantin

Granada ®
Granada Publishing ®

To Nellie

Contents

1 Rebecca's Ambition   9
2 Settling into Court House   19
3 Robbie Behaves Badly   28
4 Mara's New Dress   38
5 Invitations to the Dance   48
6 A Car Disappears   57
7 Tennis Rivals   66
8 A Dramatic Telephone Call   74
9 The Six Investigate   82
10 Looking after Robbie   93
11 Rebecca v. Madeleine   103
12 The Ultimatum   112
13 David has the Last Word   117

1
Rebecca's Ambition

'I'm not interested in boys,' said Rebecca Mason before they went back to school. She was bouncing a ball up and down on her racket. 'I'm going to stick to tennis. You won't catch me going to those dances and things and mixing with the boys from Garth College.'

'Nor me,' said Ishbel Anderson, who was called Tish for short. 'It's bad enough having a brother there.'

As juniors at Trebizon, a boarding school in the west country, they had led a fairly sheltered existence. But this term Rebecca and her friends were going up into the middle school – and would be allowed more social life. Garth College was a boys' boarding school nearby and a lot of the Trebizon girls had brothers there. (Robbie Anderson went there and so did Sue Murdoch's two brothers, David and Edward.) A certain amount of intermingling went on at weekends, but that prospect didn't interest Rebecca very much.

Tennis was her big interest in life these days ... for a good reason!

Her home was in south London but she'd actually been born in the west country – in the same county as Trebizon itself. This accident of birth qualified her for a new county scheme for junior players. Last term while she'd been playing tennis at school she had been spotted by Mrs Seabrook (the county tennis scout down there) and picked for the junior reserve squad, a group of eight boys and girls who were to have special training through the winter months. The very best of them might get promoted to the County Junior 'D' squad at Christmas.

For the summer holidays, Mrs Seabrook had arranged for Rebecca to join a tennis club near her London home. *She has a natural talent for the game and great speed around the court*, she had written to Mr and Mrs Mason, *but she is entering tennis late and has a lot of ground to make up*. Rebecca had played at the club almost every day and taken tennis lessons as well. She also practised her strokes for hours on end against the high brick wall at the back of their London house. She was making progress at an unprecedented rate.

But there was something on her mind, as Tish discovered when she rang her up towards the end of the summer holidays and invited her to stay.

'Oh, Tish, I'd love to come to your house! I've never been! But –'

'But what?'

'It's my tennis. They've put me into the Trebizon Open Tournament next Sunday. Mum and Dad are driving me back to school two days early, because Mrs Seabrook thinks I should be in it.'

'You must be getting good!' exclaimed Tish. 'Robbie goes in for that. Hey!' She suddenly realized something. 'If you're going back early you can get two really good rooms in Court House, before anyone arrives! One for us three, you and me and Sue, and one for –'

'– the other three. Margot and Mara and Elf!' Rebecca smiled down the phone. 'I'd already thought of that!'

'Anyway, what's the problem?' Tish asked. 'That's not till next weekend, so what's to stop you coming here for a few days first?'

'The problem is my tennis. It's awful. And guess who my partner's going to be in the tournament?'

'Bjorn Borg?'

'Shut up, Tish!' laughed Rebecca. 'It's nearly as bad. Someone called David Driscoll. He's part of the county tennis set-up. He's the man who's going to be teaching our group! I'm dreading it ...'

'Well, why not come here and dread it in comfort?' Tish enquired.

'I dunno, Tish ...' Rebecca felt torn. 'I'd *so* like to come. But I daren't stop practising. I've joined this club, you see, and we've got this big wall at the back of the house –'

'But we've got our own tennis court!' exclaimed Tish, now that she understood. 'Didn't I ever tell you?'

'No!' Rebecca was amazed.

'And Robbie can coach you!'

'Robbie – your brother?'

'Yes. He's really good – he wins all the tennis cups at Garth. He's working on a farm in the afternoons but he's here in the mornings. He'll help you. Say you'll come! Ask your parents – ring back!'

'You bet!' said Rebecca.

That conversation had taken place on Sunday.

Now it was Tuesday morning. Rebecca was standing outside the gate of the Andersons' hard tennis court, discussing school with Tish while waiting for her first tennis lesson with Robbie.

She could see him in the distance, rear view only, slim hips and long legs clad in old denim trousers. His head was under the bonnet of an elderly black saloon parked round the back of the house. Helen, Tish's elder sister, was standing beside him. He'd said he would only be a tick – but it was turning out to be a very long one.

'Oh dear,' said Tish. 'Helen's asked him to fix her car before she drives back to London. He'll be hours. He's crazy about cars – he can't wait for the day when he'll be old enough to have a licence.'

'Oh,' said Rebecca.

In the distance, the engine gave a sudden loud roar. Robbie slammed down the bonnet, spoke quickly to Helen and then ran and jumped into the driving seat.

'Helen's letting him drive it!' exclaimed Tish. 'Oh, she's stupid. She always lets him get round her.'

Sure enough the car reversed, then turned, then mounted the expanse of bumpy rough grass that lay between the back of the house and the tennis court. The next moment it was bumping and jolting slowly over the tussocks towards them.

'But he's not old enough to have a licence!' said Rebecca, alarmed.

'He doesn't need one, as long as he stays in our grounds,' said Tish. 'He's been practising since he was thirteen.

Nobody's car's safe when Robbie's around!'

'Is he going to run us over?'

'Shouldn't think so!' grinned Tish.

Robbie braked hard alongside them and wound the window down. His black curly hair stood on end, there was a smear of oil on his forehead and he was smiling happily.

'Sorry, Rebecca!' he shouted above the engine noise. 'Just got to get a bit of driving in before Helen goes. Won't be long. You two have a knock up!'

He revved up the engine and then the car went lurching off around the outside of the tennis court and through an open gate that led into the paddock beyond, honking loudly. Half a dozen young ewes, Dr Anderson's pride and joy, at once stopped their peaceful grazing, picked up their short little legs and wobbled away as fast as they could go, all in a huddle, baaa-ing crossly, until they reached the hedge in the far corner of the paddock. They then resumed their grazing beneath a spreading oak tree, a safe and secluded spot.

'Lunatic!' said Tish. 'Come on, let's play.'

They opened the gate of the tennis court and went inside, wound the net up to its correct height and then started to knock the ball backwards and forwards. Rebecca thought that the sound of the ball thwacking against racket strings was one of the nicest sounds on earth and she began to feel very happy.

'Rebeck!' exclaimed Tish, racing to retrieve a forehand and only just getting it back. 'Wow! What's happened to you?'

Rebecca was already up at the net and put Tish's loose return away with an angled backhand volley. She couldn't help laughing at the expression on Tish's face. Tish was a very sound player and even three months ago could have beaten Rebecca easily. Now she was flabbergasted.

'Have I improved?'

'Improved. It's amazing!'

They settled down to a hard knock-up, pelting the balls backwards and forwards. Out of the corner of her eye, Rebecca could see across the hedge and into the paddock. The battered old black car roared round and round the field, bucking and roaring over the bumpy patches. Each time the car came close to the hedge she could glimpse Robbie, hunched over the steering wheel, the breeze from the window blowing his hair around, a look of glazed ecstasy on his face. Then with a great deal of brrrrmphing and revving and gear changing, he would take the car into a tight U-turn and brrroooommmmm off across the field again.

'Does he ever hit anything?' she called out to Tish.

'Not very often!' replied Tish, sending up a high lob.

A moment later there came a screech of brakes and a tremendous juddering sound as Robbie, coming up to the hedge and turning too late, had to stop dead.

'Oh, no!' said Tish.

The car slid forward, before Robbie could stop it, and gently nose-dived into the wide ditch that ran beneath the hedge.

Glancing back towards the house, Rebecca caught a glimpse of Helen's pale face at an upstairs window. She seemed to be waving her arms.

Robbie switched off the engine and climbed out of the car, shouting through the hedge in the direction of the tennis court.

'Quick, you two, come and help!'

Rebecca and Tish ran round into the paddock and tried hard not to laugh at the sight of the car, its front wheels hanging down in the ditch. No damage had been done.

'Come on, help me push it out before Helen sees!' said Robbie, already down in the ditch and getting his shoulder under the front bumper. 'She gets excited.'

14

'She has seen,' Tish stated calmly. 'And she may be excited already.'

Luckily Robbie was tall and strong. With the three of them heaving and lifting and puffing, they had the car safely out of the ditch by the time Helen arrived. She was smartly dressed and wearing high-heeled shoes, ready to drive back to her flat in London.

'Is everything all right?' she asked suspiciously.

'Fine!' said Robbie nonchalantly, though his face was still red from his exertions. 'I've given it a good run and the timing's okay. It was just the plugs. They were filthy.'

'I don't see why you have to drive it so fast,' said Helen. 'I think I'd better take it now.'

'Okay.' Robbie looked disappointed. 'Let me just put it back on the drive for you.' He jumped into the driving seat quickly, before Helen could refuse, and held open the passenger door for her. They reversed and then went slowly and very soberly off through the paddock gate. Rebecca and Tish walked along behind.

They watched as Robbie parked the car on the back drive. While Helen went into the house to get her overnight bag, he got out a handkerchief and polished the windscreen for her, although it was already perfectly clean.

'Robbie!' yelled Tish, cupping her hands to her mouth. 'Rebecca's waiting!'

Robbie shoved the handkerchief in his pocket, surveyed the car once more and then tore himself away.

'Coming!' he shouted. 'Got my racket there?'

As Robbie ambled slowly and dreamily across the grass towards them, every so often glancing back at the car as though he were saying good-bye to it, Tish whispered to Rebecca:

'Some car or other will get Robbie into a whole lot of trouble one day!'

Rebecca had a marvellous time at the Andersons' house. It was fun being with Tish again, and they wished that Sue, the other member of their trio, could have been there, too. But they would soon be reunited – the autumn term at Trebizon was less than a week away now!

Rebecca began to lose some of her nerves about playing in the Trebizon Open Tournament on Sunday. Robbie was a very good player indeed and he played with her every morning, making her work like a slave on some of her weaker strokes.

'If you do make mistakes, your partner will cover up for you,' said Robbie. 'It's not as though it's a singles tournament. As a matter of fact you're much better than the girl I'm going to be playing with.' He said that quite happily and Rebecca wondered who the girl was. 'Have they found someone good to play with you, Rebeck?'

'Yes,' said Rebecca. 'He's a county tennis coach – a new one. He's going to be teaching our group this winter! He *must* be good, that's why I'm scared. I hope he won't get annoyed with me.'

'What's his name? Maybe I know him.'

'David Driscoll,' said Rebecca.

Recognition crossed Robbie's face.

'Oh, yes. Driscoll. He *is* good. He's a Trebizon boy – lives in the town.'

'Boy?' said Rebecca, in surprise.

'Well, "young man" then. He was at Trebizon Tech. but I think he left this summer. He plays county tennis – senior level – drives a little moped everywhere. He was hoping to get a job in export, somebody told me, but it must have fallen through if he's hanging around doing tennis coaching.'

'Do you know him well then?' Rebecca asked.

'No! Played against him, that's all. Garth has regular tennis fixtures with Trebizon Tech. Every time we've met he's beaten me.'

16

'But he must be older than you!' said Rebecca, tactfully.

'Three years,' said Robbie. Then he gave his wide smile, so reminiscent of Tish's. 'It's not a very high-powered tournament on Sunday. With luck I'll get to the finals. What's the betting that you and David get to the finals, too – and beat me and Virginia?'

'Who's Virginia?' Rebecca asked Tish, later.

'Virginia Slade,' said Tish.

'Oh!' said Rebecca. 'I know.'

Virginia Slade was at Trebizon and was two years older than they were – a pretty girl with a mass of little blonde bubble curls. She was a senior in Court House, the same boarding house that the six friends in III Alpha were going into. It seemed that her father was Robbie's housemaster at Garth College – which was how Robbie had got to know her.

'It's going to be embarrassing having Robbie hanging around Court at the weekends,' said Tish gloomily.

'Why, is he keen on her then?' asked Rebecca.

'Besotted! Half the boys in his house are. Apparently when she goes to help her mother do the teas for house matches they flock round the tea urn all afternoon. Suddenly get wildly interested in the stuff.'

'I can just imagine,' said Rebecca. She could feel another spot coming up on her chin and rubbed it. 'But she must like Robbie if she's playing with him on Sunday. She must like him more than the rest.'

'She likes playing with someone who's good!' said Tish cynically. 'I think that's all there is to it. But he's struck a hard bargain. In return for being her partner on Sunday, she's got to let him take her to the Hallowe'en Dance!'

'What, the one that's held at our school?'

'That's right,' said Tish. 'We'll be allowed to go to it this year if we want to. We're considered big girls now!

17

If you don't know any boys, you put your name down on a list and your housemistress scrapes up a partner for you!'

'No *thanks*!' said Rebecca.

After lunch on Friday it was time for Rebecca to return home. She went to find Robbie. He was round the back of the house, wearing old clothes and pumping up his bicycle tyres, ready to go to work for the last time. He'd earned a lot of money these holidays apparently and put it all in Post Office savings towards what he called his 'car fund'. Rebecca was amazed at such dedication as it would be a long time before he could actually buy an old car and drive it on the roads.

He stopped pumping and looked up and smiled at her.

'Going?'

'Yes. I just wanted to say thanks,' said Rebecca, shyly. 'It's been boring for you, but for me it's been a big help – I don't feel half so nervous now.'

'It hasn't been boring,' said Robbie, shortly. He returned to his pumping. 'You're going to be really good soon. They'll be putting you in one of the county squads before you know it.'

Rebecca turned away quickly, a tingling feeling going down her spine.

Ten minutes later, Tish pushed her on board the Green Line bus that would take her back through the Hertfordshire villages and into London.

'Don't forget to find two rooms together! Good luck on Sunday! See you Monday. 'Bye!'

Rebecca waved until Tish was out of sight. Court House was going to be fun! And did Robbie really mean it, did he know what he was talking about? The County Junior 'D' Squad after Christmas – was it possible?

Of course not. It was a dream. She mustn't even think about it.

2

Settling into Court House

On Saturday morning Rebecca said good-bye to the ter-
raced house in south London, near the common. It would
be nearly a year before she saw it again. It had been a happy
time, living in her own home again for two months, having

her parents back. But now her father's leave was almost up. He and her mother were due to return to Saudi Arabia and the house would be let furnished until next summer.

She had come to regard Trebizon as a kind of substitute home. The thought had once filled her with horror – but not any longer. So far, her parents had never even been there. She had always travelled there alone by train or bus. The Masons had had to send her to a boarding school rather hurriedly last year when her father had been posted abroad. They could never have afforded to send her to a famous school themselves, but the firm was paying all the fees. Now they were going to see Trebizon at last!

They drove down to the west country in the hired car, with Rebecca's trunk on board, even fuller than usual. Now that she and Tish and Sue were going to share their own study-bedroom in Court House, instead of being in a dormitory in Juniper, the junior house, there would be room for ornaments and one or two posters and some favourite books.

It was a golden September afternoon when they reached the town of Trebizon, still sprinkled with holidaymakers, the cafés and souvenir shops in the main street gay with summer awnings. They climbed out of the town and along the top road, past hotels and little palm trees, the glittering blue of Trebizon Bay in the distance. Then in through the main gates of the school, driving slowly through parkland, until the fine old manor house that formed the heart of the school came into view.

'Oh, Becky!' said Mrs Mason. 'It's even nicer than the photos.'

'Lovely place,' grunted Mr Mason. 'And that's the sea isn't it – through the trees?'

Rebecca was pleased that they were seeing it at its best.

'Let's drive straight round to Court House!' she said eagerly. 'Look – fork right here by the rhododendrons, there's a track that cuts straight through.'

The car plunged down the track. Lush foliage brushed against the windows and the air was full of scents. They caught a brief glimpse of the Hilary Camberwell Music School, its Spanish-style buildings fronting on to a small lake, and then they drew up in front of a rambling old house covered in Virginia creeper.

'We're here!' exclaimed Rebecca, climbing out of the car.

'Rebecca!' shrieked a voice.

The front door of Court House was open and a pretty girl with sandy coloured hair and glasses came rushing out with her arms outflung.

'Sue!' yelled Rebecca, hugging her. 'What on earth are you doing here!'

'Never mind that! What on earth are *you* doing here –?'

They were laughing, twirling round, both talking at once.

'Tish said you were at a Music Festival all this week!'

'I was and it's over and here I am! Mr and Mrs Barrington brought me back with them this morning. It was in Plymouth – it would have been crazy for me to go all the way back to London, just for two days. But what are *you* –?'

Rebecca explained.

'Honestly?' said Sue. 'Tomorrow's tournament! You mean to say you're *in* it!'

They talked nineteen to the dozen. Rebecca introduced her parents. They took to Sue straight away, she could tell.

'Well, your mother and I had better go and look for Mrs Barrington and see about your trunk and getting you settled in,' said Mr Mason, glad to stretch his legs after the long drive. 'Where do I find her, Sue?'

'The Barringtons live in that wing of the house over there,' said Sue, pointing. 'That's their own private front door, the blue one, with their car parked outside it. I think Mrs Barrington's round the back, putting some washing out.'

Mr Barrington was the Director of Music at Trebizon and his wife Joan was the housemistress in charge of the thirty-six girls who lived in Court House. She also taught art.

'Come on, Sue!' said Rebecca, as her parents went off.

They ran into the main part of the house. The entrance hall was spacious and smelt pleasantly of floor polish. There was a sofa and a wide pinewood staircase and a coin-box telephone fixed to the wall. There were lots of hooks for coats, some potted plants on a table and well-worn rugs scattered around the floor. The doors were solid, polished pine ones with brass door knobs. Through an open one, Rebecca could see a common room with chintzy armchairs. She felt at home at once.

'So this is Court! It's as nice inside as it is out!' she said in delight.

'I didn't know which two rooms to save!' said Sue. 'There are four empty ones for the twelve of us coming in and they're all about the same – three beds in each.'

The twelve new girls entering Court House were the A–Ms in Form III Alpha. The remaining six girls in III Alpha, the N–Zs, were going into Norris House. Luckily Rebecca and her five friends were all A–Ms!

'Well us six have got to be near each other, that's the main thing.' Rebecca glanced towards the staircase. 'Let's go up and see the rooms!'

'We can't!' laughed Sue. 'They're on the ground floor. We're at the bottom of the middle school so we have to be at the bottom of the house, too, where everyone can keep an eye on us! Next year, when we're Fourth Years, we move up to the first floor which is a bit more private.'

'And the year after?' enquired Rebecca.

'Up to the attic rooms – really cosy and tucked away

22

on their own. The Fifth Years have got it made up there! It's dead quiet and you can see right across to old school and the sea beyond that.' Sue had been having a good look round! 'Of course it's Certificate year so they need to have some peace and quiet to swot for their exams.'

'So that's the system!' said Rebecca, fascinated. 'We start at the bottom and work our way up. Always something better to look forward to.'

'It's much better already!' said Sue. 'Much better than it was in the dormitory. Come and see.'

The four study-bedrooms were down a little corridor that led off the main hall and were all very similar in size and layout. They were identically furnished. Each held three beds, three chests of drawers, three chairs, a clothes cupboard and a homework table.

The difference was that two overlooked the front gardens of the house and the other two overlooked a very big courtyard at the back, all mellow flagstones and sunshine. The Barringtons' tabby cat was sunning herself on a low wall there. As the four rooms were close together anyway, it was the view that clinched it. After much discussion Rebecca and Sue decided that they preferred to overlook the back and that Tish would, too. Mara and Elf and Margot would feel the same way!

'Yes, it's more interesting out of this window!' said Sue, dragging her trunk in from the corridor. 'Thank goodness that's decided!'

Not only was the courtyard warm and friendly looking, with washing billowing and hens clucking around, but they could see directly across to Norris House, the other boarding house, where the remaining six girls in III Alpha and six III Beta girls would be living. It consisted of a long row of stone buildings, once outbuildings to Court House but now converted into attractive living quarters. The buildings backed on to the same courtyard, on the far side of it.

'We'll be able to see Joss going out jogging in the morning!' said Rebecca, gazing out of the window. 'And maybe Roberta and Debbie and the twins practising their plays ... oh, Sue! Isn't it great to be first here so we can take our pick!'

They all had tea in the Barringtons' part of the house and then Mr Barrington showed Rebecca's parents round the main school buildings and the grounds while the girls unpacked and made the room look cosy. After that Mr Mason treated them to dinner at the Seaview Hotel, where he and Mrs Mason were booked in for the night, and then drove them back to Court House.

'You'd better get some sleep, Becky,' he said, kissing her on the cheek. 'You've got your tournament tomorrow and your mother and I have come a long way to watch you. My word, I like your room! You've got your posters up already! Is that your violin, Sue?'

It was some time before Rebecca and Sue got to sleep. There was so much to talk about.

'I just can't wait to see what David Driscoll's like tomorrow!' said Rebecca long after they'd put the lights out. 'I hope Robbie's right and he'll cover up for all my mistakes. Oh, Sue, I've got butterflies in my stomach ...'

'I always get those, just before I have to play in a concert,' said Sue. 'Don't worry, Rebecca. It'll be all right ...'

There was a light tap on the door. 'Shut up, you two —' Mrs Barrington called out cheerfully, '– and go to sleep!'

The housemistress supplied them with bacon and eggs and the two girls cooked themselves a huge Sunday breakfast in the boarding house kitchen. It was at the back of the house and had big windows and a french door that opened on to the courtyard. 'Stoke up, Rebecca,' Mrs Barrington had warned. 'You'll only get a cold lunch today and the tennis goes on for hours.'

The Trebizon Open Tournament was a mixed doubles

contest organized by tennis enthusiasts in the town. The town didn't have enough courts to accommodate it and so it was always held at Trebizon School by kind permission of the principal, at the very end of the summer holidays, just before the tennis nets were taken down and the netball posts put up for winter. The tournament started at ten and went on all day, with a light lunch provided by the school at so much per head. All mixed double pairs in each half of the tournament played everyone in their half during the course of the day. They added up their scores at the end and then the top-scoring pair from each half played the final.

'I'm glad it isn't a knock-out tournament,' said Rebecca. 'Imagine how my partner would feel if I let us get knocked out in the first round.'

'Shouldn't think there would have been much danger of that,' said Sue, piling some of Mrs Barrington's homemade marmalade on to buttered toast. 'Mmmm. This tastes good. From what you say, he sounds so brilliant that all you have to do is to keep out of the way of the ball –'

'Hope so!' murmured Rebecca.

'– and dance around the court and look glamorous. I like your tennis dress, Rebecca. Where did you get it?'

Suddenly there was a spluttering, putt-putting sound as a moped was driven into the courtyard and up to the kitchen. The engine stopped and there came a firm rap on the back door.

'Hallo?'

Sue opened the door and saw a very crisp young man in tennis whites standing there. He was muscular, of medium height, with straight brown hair neatly combed and parted. His clothes were so dazzling white they looked like a washing powder advert. There were two tennis rackets clipped to his moped.

'Pleased to meet you,' he said in a west country accent,

shaking hands with Sue. He had a very precise manner. 'I'm David Driscoll. You must be Miss Mason.'

'No, I'm Sue Murdoch –' She pushed Rebecca forward. 'This is Rebecca.'

'Hallo,' said Rebecca shyly.

David Driscoll smiled at her.

'They said I'd find you here. I'll call you Rebecca, if you don't mind and you call me David. Surnames are rather formal.'

'Of – of course,' said Rebecca. She thought that although he was trying not to be, he was surprisingly formal anyway! It made him seem older than he was.

'I suggest we go straight to the courts and have a knock-up now, Rebecca,' he said. 'I'd like to get an idea of your standard.'

'Go on!' said Sue quickly, as Rebecca hesitated, 'I'll wash up the breakfast things and wait here for your parents – you go and get your tennis racket.'

'Do you mind if I leave my moped here till this evening?' said David.

They walked out through the front hall and almost collided with a girl rushing in. She wore a white tennis dress and had small blonde curls and a very pretty face. Her arms were laden with clothes.

'David!' she squealed. 'Hallo!'

'Hallo, Virginia. Feeling fit?'

'Good heavens no. I shall leave all the fast balls to Robbie Anderson. Daddy's brought us both over from Garth in his new car – it's outside, you should see it! I'm just going to dump these clothes up in my room, ready for the new term. 'Bye!'

They went out of the front door and walked along the track away from Court House. Rebecca looked around but couldn't see any sign of a car or of Robbie. Then she heard his voice.

'Rebeck!'

'Hallo, Robbie!' she called, waving.

She could just glimpse him through a gap in the hedge. Mr Slade's car was parked, not in front of Court House, but round the side – in the Barringtons' private area, near their front door. Robbie's housemaster had obviously gone inside to say hallo. Robbie had climbed out of the car while he was waiting in order to stand back and look at it.

'What a car!' gasped Rebecca. Even to her eyes, it was the most graceful thing she had ever seen. A long, low silver sports car, dazzling new and shining, the sun glinting on it here and there. 'Is that Mr Slade's new car?'

'Must be,' shrugged David Driscoll.

'See you down at the courts!' called Robbie, his gaze at once returning to the car. He was running a hand along the bonnet, stroking it reverently.

Rebecca and David walked on.

'I don't know where some people get the money,' was all he said.

'No,' confessed Rebecca. 'Nor do I.'

He glanced at her briefly and gave a nod, as though he approved of her. But only one thing mattered to Rebecca at that moment. The tennis tournament – the very first one she had ever played in! – was only half an hour away. She gripped her racket tightly and wondered what it was going to be like playing with a county senior player – and her future coach.

3
Robbie Behaves Badly

It ought to have been terrifying, but it wasn't. It was exhilarating. Rebecca realized afterwards that with a partner like David Driscoll it could hardly have been anything else. He completely outshone everyone in their half of the tournament at Trebizon that day. He was always there, covering the court, if she missed a shot. As they won game after game, Rebecca's confidence grew. She found her touch, served well and made a lot of good shots from the baseline. But her partner, volleying and smashing, would have devastated the opposition anyway.

'Whatever were you worrying about?' laughed Sue, when they broke off for lunch. They went to the main school dining hall. She and Rebecca piled their plates high with salad and cold meats from the buffet and then went out into the sunshine to join Mr and Mrs Mason on the terrace. 'Isn't she fantastic?' Sue asked Rebecca's parents.

'Her tennis has come on, hasn't it?' said Mr Mason, proudly. Before lunch he'd noted down all the totals on the scoreboard. 'Looks like we're going to have to wait and see the final! How can they fail to get in it?'

'We will wait, won't we, love?' asked Mrs Mason anxiously. 'I don't care how late we get back to London tonight! The car doesn't have to be back tonight does it?'

'Tomorrow morning!' said Mr Mason. 'We're not going to miss this!'

'It's nothing to do with me!' laughed Rebecca. 'It's all David.' She felt on top of the world. There were people everywhere, balancing plates, eating, laughing, talking. She had been getting glances from some of the towns-people in the course of the morning.

Who's that girl with the long fair hair playing with David Driscoll?

She's quite good, isn't she? One of the Trebizon girls, I think.

She didn't play here last year did she? Don't remember her.

During lunch a very tall lady in a cream linen suit and floppy hat came over and joined them. She was the county tennis scout and one look at Rebecca's glowing face was enough.

'I can see you're enjoying it,' Mrs Seabrook smiled. 'I decided to throw you in at the deep end.' She turned to Rebecca's parents and introduced herself. They had exchanged letters but never met. 'How did it go for Rebecca in the holidays?'

They discussed the county training scheme and Rebecca's tennis in general. Rebecca and Sue slipped away. They took the empty plates back to the dining hall and got some chocolate cake. Tish's brother was in there, steering Virginia towards the coffee. He gave them a cheerful wave.

'I wonder what *their* scores are like?' Rebecca suddenly wondered. 'They're in the other half.'

'They're well ahead,' replied Sue. They walked back out into the sunshine. 'Tish ought to be here! It's obvious you four are going to meet in the final – it's going to be exciting! Except – poor Tish – she wouldn't know which side to cheer for!'

'Then maybe it's just as well she's not!' laughed Rebecca. But there was a churning feeling in her stomach. 'Robbie said we might meet in the final – he said it the other day – I thought he was joking. But David's so good ... Sue! It's just beginning to sink in. The final! I wonder who's going to win –?'

'You and David, of course,' said Sue. Then, loyally, because she liked Tish's brother: 'But Robbie's good. It won't be a walkover.'

Rebecca shivered with excitement. It was proving to be a great day! Even the weather was perfect. Nothing could spoil a day like today, thought Rebecca. But she was wrong.

Something could spoil it, just a little, and it did.

She and David got to the final. So did Robbie and Virginia. It would be played at four o'clock – the best of three

30

sets. At five minutes to four, David took her over to the court. Up to now the tournament had been very informal, with players keeping their own scores and retrieving their own balls. The final would be different, with ballboys, linesmen and an umpire sitting up in a high chair. A grey-haired gentleman, president of the tennis club in the town, was climbing up into the umpire's chair now. Lots of people were drifting over and sitting down on the high banks behind the tennis courts to get a good view of the match. Rebecca's parents were there, with Sue, and so was Miss Sara Willis who was in charge of games at Trebizon and lived in a small cottage in the grounds. Mrs Seabrook, the county scout, had been going to leave early but had been persuaded to stay and present the silver cup at the end. It stood on a small table just inside the courts.

'Nervous, Rebecca?' asked David Driscoll.

'A bit,' she replied.

'Don't be,' he said.

Robbie and Virginia were coming out on to the court now, to join them. He was carrying her racket for her and had an arm round her shoulders. She looked slim and very pretty in her tennis dress. Robbie looked crumpled and untidy – unlike David whose whites were still immaculate after several hours' play. Robbie's dark curly hair was standing on end and he looked, Rebecca though, extremely happy.

Within a matter of seconds, all that changed. It happened when the introductions took place.

'Virginia – you know Rebecca, of course?'

'Yes.' The older girl gave Rebecca a friendly smile. 'You've moved up into Court now haven't you?'

'And this is David Driscoll –' Robbie continued. David was bending down, tying a lace. 'I don't think you've met –'

'Of course we have!' laughed Virginia, as David stood up. 'Hallo David! Where did you get to at lunch time?

I was looking for you.' She spared Robbie a brief glance. 'David's been giving me some coaching these holidays. I've been dying to talk to him all day.'

She put a hand on the older boy's arm and gazed at him, rather flirtatiously, Rebecca thought. 'David – my serve – the way you showed me. It's really beginning to work.'

'Good,' said David, shortly.

Robbie was glowering and the atmosphere had suddenly become rather icy. But Virginia didn't even notice that Robbie was jealous. She continued to gaze at David.

'Don't you dare play really fiercely,' she said, pouting but looking very pretty at the same time. 'This is only a friendly little tournament. Give Robbie and me a chance!'

'Don't be silly,' snapped Robbie.

Rebecca glanced at him uneasily. It might have been a friendly little tournament up to a few seconds ago. As far as Robbie Anderson was concerned, it wasn't any longer. He'd show Virginia – even if he had to run himself into the ground!

He stormed through the first five games, keeping Virginia off the ball, playing to David all the time as though it were a men's singles! His mouth was set in a hard line and he played with a concentration and ferocity that took them quite by surprise. In no time at all, David and Rebecca were 1–4 down and in danger of losing the first set!

As they changed ends, a hum of conversation ran through the onlookers. Things had taken an unexpected turn! Which way was the match going to go? Young Robbie Anderson was playing some inspired tennis.

But David Driscoll was completely unruffled.

'I think I'd better sharpen up a bit, Rebecca,' he said, calmly. 'You've had a very long day. I don't want it to go to three sets. Let's stop the rot.'

He began to play with great precision and control, taking the steam out of Robbie with long, punishing rallies that slowed down the pace and then suddenly closing in to the net with whiplash volleys to score. Virginia gave gasps of admiration at some of those points.

'Whose side are you on?' asked Robbie fiercely at one stage and Rebecca could see that he was getting angry and frustrated.

The score in games levelled to 4–4, the next game was crucial.

Virginia was serving and she and Robbie were 30–40 down.

The first serve was in. David cracked it back on the forehand and then Robbie countered with a sizzling backhand into the tramlines. Rebecca showed how fast she could move by racing over and getting the tip of her racket to it sending it, back in a high lob.

Robbie ran backwards, waiting for the ball to drop, then smashed hard towards the baseline.

'Out!' called the linesman.

'Game to Driscoll and Miss Mason, 5 games to 4 –' began the umpire.

'It was in!' shouted Robbie furiously. 'It hit the baseline – I saw it –' He walked over to the umpire's chair, still protesting. 'It was in – the score should be deuce.'

The umpire glanced towards the linesman who shook his head stubbornly, although in fact he had made a bad call.

'Out. Game to Driscoll –'

'It was in!' Robbie continued to argue and gesticulate and point to the baseline. In the crowd, somebody booed.

Stop it, Robbie! thought Rebecca.

David Driscoll kept perfectly calm.

'He's making a fool of himself,' he stated. 'As if it matters! He thinks he's at Wimbledon.'

'It matters to him,' she said, loyally.

The umpire ordered Robbie back on to the court and

33

David and Rebecca went on to win the first set, 6–4.

Robbie was completely unsettled after that. In the second set some more hairsbreadth decisions went against him and at one stage he actually threw his racket down on to the court in a fury. Somebody started up a slow handclap until, red-faced and apologizing to the umpire, he picked up his racket and got on with the game.

Rebecca wanted to sink into the ground with shame for him. It upset her own game. But Robbie's antics didn't have the slightest effect on David Driscoll. He was quite unruffled – and proceeded to dominate the match. They won the second set 6–1 and it was all over.

'Game, set and match to Driscoll and Miss Mason.'

They all shook hands at the net. 'You were in good form, David,' said Virginia, admiration written all over her face. She gave him a playful push. 'Go and get your cup, then.'

'I want my partner to have it,' said David. To Rebecca's surprise he put an arm round her shoulders. 'Her first tennis trophy – I don't think it will be her last.'

Mrs Seabrook presented Rebecca with the cup and then shook hands with all four players. The onlookers clapped politely, except for Sue who gave a loud cheer. Rebecca knew that her part in winning the tournament had been a minor one, but it was a wonderful moment all the same. She walked towards the court gate intending to find Sue and her parents, and show them the cup.

Robbie got there first and held open the gate for her. 'I'm sorry, Rebeck,' he said. He mustered a smile as he looked at the cup. 'Don't let Tish use it for lemonade.' But she knew that he was feeling ashamed of himself and miserable.

'Don't worry, Robbie.' Rebecca gave him her best smile. 'I won't.'

His eyes had already strayed back to Virginia, who was chatting to David Driscoll. Rebecca hurried off.

Margaret Exton, an old enemy of Tish's, barred her

way. She had arrived back at school this afternoon, a day early, because her father was buying up a sports car factory in the west country.

'Tish Anderson's brother behaved like a big ape,' she said loudly.

Rebecca pushed past her and joined her parents and Sue. There was much hugging and back slapping. They held the cup and admired it. 'But I thought your friend Tish's brother behaved rather badly,' said Mrs Mason. Miss Willis came over and joined them and then David Driscoll wandered up.

'Well, David, what do you think of her?' The games mistress knew the new part-time coach by sight. 'Do you think she deserves her place in the reserve squad? When do your training sessions start?'

'A fortnight's time. I think we'll be able to do quite a lot with her.' His manner was still formal, but he looked at Rebecca approvingly. 'My moped's over at the boarding house. I'd better get it. Can anyone remind me how to get back there?'

'I –' Rebecca felt that the question was directed at her, but she wished he hadn't asked it. She was still thinking about Robbie Anderson. Where was he? Was he still feeling awful? She wanted to see him!

'Sue –' said Miss Willis quickly, '– take David back to Court House.'

Soon it was time for Mr and Mrs Mason to drive back to London.

Their suitcase was packed and their car was parked up by the main school building. When Rebecca took her parents up there, she saw an admiring crowd gathered around the sleek silver car that was parked next to it. Mr Slade was sitting at the wheel. He had returned, to collect Virginia for her last night at home and at the same time to give Robbie a lift back to school.

Suddenly Virginia rushed past them, tugging Robbie

35

along by the shirt-sleeve. 'Come on, Daddy's waiting! I'd better not tell him about the stew you got into!' She gave a little laugh. 'Silly Robbie!'

Rebecca watched them go by and she sighed.

It didn't seem to bother Virginia that Robbie had made a fool of himself!

It didn't even seem to bother him any longer. He looked happy enough.

Let David Driscoll putt-putt off home, thought Robbie. Right now he was going to be driven back to Garth College with Virginia – in old Slade's new car!

He opened the gleaming door and helped her in and then got in beside her and slammed it shut. He stared, mesmerized at the magnificent instrument panel. What a car! And what a girl! Roll on the Dance. Pity it wasn't until right at the end of October. He could think of several boys who would pester her about it. But she'd promised *him* – Robbie Anderson – and that was settled!

Virginia was thinking: *Robbie's sweet. But I think I'm going off boys of my own age. I think I prefer them David's age.*

John Slade started up the engine and let in the clutch. In his imagination so did Robbie. Smooth, skilful. They were moving away ...

'Good-bye, Robbie!' Rebecca burst out.

He saw her, through a blur.

'Good-bye!'

She wouldn't be seeing him again until the night of the Hallowe'en Dance.

'The ball was definitely in,' said Sue, as they lay in their beds talking that night. 'But I've never known Robbie be a bad sport before. I don't know what came over him.'

'He was just desperate to win. He was trying to impress Virginia, of course,' said Rebecca. That was the part she didn't want to think about.

'He must have it bad,' said Sue. She yawned loudly.

'Tish will be furious,' said Rebecca. 'Margaret Exton won't let her live this down.'

'I was thinking how perfect it is here,' said Sue. 'Being in Court House.' Through a gap in the curtains she could see the moon sliding out from behind a cloud. 'You've just reminded me of the one drawback. We've got Margaret Exton.'

'Right.'

Rebecca was almost asleep. The moonlight caught the edge of the silver cup standing on her chest of drawers, and made it shimmer. It had been a great day. A day to remember. It was a pity that something had happened to spoil it, just a little.

She had woken up thinking about David Driscoll, but she went to sleep thinking about Robbie Anderson.

4
Mara's New Dress

Woomph! Whooomph! Thwack! Whooomph! Forehand,
backhand, smash, volley! Rebecca was playing tennis
against herself, pounding the ball at the wall relentlessly.
The blank end wall of Norris House across the courtyard,

with its smooth area of paving stones in front, made the perfect practice place.

Today was Monday September 7th and all boarders were due back. Girls had been arriving in cars throughout the afternoon and the coaches had gone to Trebizon station to meet the train girls. Tish would be here soon – and Margot and Elf! Mara would come by road. To the Greek girl's deep regret she was never allowed to travel by train on her own. Mr Leonodis was one of the world's richest men. He adored his youngest daughter and didn't believe in taking unnecessary risks.

Sue was over in the Hilary, practising her violin, and Rebecca was busy sharpening up her reflexes, hitting ball after ball, non-stop.

'Congratulations Rebecca!' shouted Josselyn Vining, coming out of Norris with some damp washing. She hung her track suit and games socks on the line to dry. She'd been playing in a seven-a-side hockey tournament at Clifford, where she lived, before being driven straight on to school. 'Hear you won the tournie here yesterday!'

'Not me, Joss!' Rebecca shouted back, going at full stretch as the ball came at a funny angle – 'Not me ... got it! ... my partner!'

She battered on, as Joss came up and watched her.

'Which days will you be going to Exonford?' She knew that Rebecca had got into the county junior reserve squad. She trained with the 'A' squad herself. 'Saturdays or Sundays?'

'Every other Saturday,' Rebecca puffed, 'starting the nineteenth.'

'Pity. Our training sessions are going to be Sundays this winter. We could have gone on the train together!'

Exonford was the only town in the county that had indoor tennis courts and training facilities. All the county schemes were based there. It was twenty miles away.

'Who was your partner yesterday?'

39

'David Driscoll,' said Rebecca, whamming another ball.

'Oh, him?' Joss played regularly for the county junior 'A' team but also, at only thirteen, had played some senior games this summer, alongside Rebecca's coach. 'All serious, isn't he?'

'Is he?' Rebecca thought for a moment. 'He's good though, isn't he? He's going to take our group.'

'You mean he's working for the county?' Joss sounded surprised. 'He told me he was trying to get a job in industry. He left Trebizon Tech. back in June with a diploma in business studies.'

'Maybe he can't find one. Maybe he's filling in time.'

All this time Rebecca had never stopped hitting the ball.

'You ought to be glad your sessions are on Sunday, Joss. You'll be needed for hockey on Saturdays.'

Joss just nodded. She was very tall with short brown curly hair and the outstanding athlete of Rebecca's year – brilliant at just about everything. She'd already played at Junior Wimbledon and next summer might enter the qualifying rounds for the senior tournament. The world-famous Wimbledon tournament! But at the same time she was already being looked upon as a future athletics prospect – and, of course, the county hockey selectors were keeping an eye on her. She was amazing – and it made her seem a little remote from the rest of them sometimes.

'Blow me, you've improved Rebecca,' she said suddenly.

'Have I?' Rebecca tried to sound casual.

'Maybe we could play sometimes?' Joss said. 'They keep the net up on the staff court all the year round.'

'Do they?' Rebecca stopped dead and caught the ball in her hand. 'You mean – where the teachers play? By the kitchen gardens? But surely not just anybody can play –'

'Who's anybody? They let you play if you've got prospects,' smiled Joss. 'I've got to dash now. Found a room for myself in Norris – got to finish unpacking. 'Bye!'

''Bye!' Rebecca swung her racket and thumped the ball against the wall with renewed vigour. Got prospects! That familiar tingling went down her spine again. Had she? Or was it all a bubble that was suddenly going to burst? What were the other boys and girls in the reserve squad going to be like ... would they be better than her when it came to it ... much, much better? Come the nineteenth, she might find out. *Whooomph. Whooomph. Thwack.* Forehand, backhand, smash!

She was soon engrossed again. She didn't hear somebody creep up behind her until suddenly – urrrmphh! – they leapt on her back and put their hands across her eyes.

'Guess who!'

'Tish!' shouted Rebecca joyfully, then grabbed her under the knees. 'Charge!'

She lowered her head and ran several yards with Tish on her back going 'Ayahahahaha' like a Red Indian, then deliberately collapsed forward towards the ground so that they landed in a tangled heap in the middle of the courtyard, laughing helplessly.

'Congratulations!' Tish smote her on the back. 'You won!'

They scrambled up.

'You know?'

'I've just seen Sue – she showed me the room, fantastic! – and she told me! How you and Driscoll beat Robbie and Virginia and how my dear brother showed me up and Margaret Exton isn't going to let me live it down! Come on, everybody's just arrived, Mara too. Sue's just going to cut her birthday cake!'

'Yippee!'

They rushed over to Court House and in through the kitchen door. There were four girls in there. Sue was back from music practice and was cutting a rich iced fruit cake that her mother had baked and packed in her trunk. She was fourteen today. Margot Lawrence was there and so were Sally Elphinstone – Elf for short – and Mara Leonodis.

Mara's brother Anestis, who had driven her to Trebizon, was out the front somewhere with the car, getting her luggage sorted out.

'Rebecca!' they all cried. The six of them were back together!

And then the other six girls from III Alpha who'd been allocated to Court House came piling into the kitchen. Aba Amori, the Nigerian girl, Anne Finch, Ann Ferguson, Jane Bowen – who, like Mara, had been promoted from the Beta stream – Elizabeth Kendall and Jenny Brook-Hayes.

'Happy birthday, Sue!'

'Let's give her the bumps!'

'Aaaaagh!' protested Sue laughing as she was lifted high in the air and then down again, fourteen times. Aaah! You stinking lot – stop it!'

There was a terrible din after that as they laughed and talked and drank coffee and ate birthday cake. In the middle of it all the door opened and the Greek boy stood there, darkly good-looking but covered in confusion, with a great frothy mass of frilled white lace in his arms. 'Mara! What do I do with *this*?'

'Anestis!' Mara laughed. 'Just put it on my bed –'

But the girls were already crowding round.

'Mara – show us!'

She took it from her brother and held it up.

'What a beautiful dress!' exclaimed Rebecca. She felt a pang of envy.

'Yes!' Mara's brown eyes were shining now. 'For the – what is it? – the All Hallows Dance.'

'Will your father let you go to that then?' asked Elf with a gulp. What wouldn't she give to be able to squeeze into a dress like that! 'I mean, isn't he strict about you meeting boys.'

'I shall be going with Anestis!' announced Mara and gave her brother a sisterly kiss on the cheek. 'Father agrees to that. Anestis has promised to come down for it. So, you see, I shall not miss any of the fun!'

Some of them looked at each other rather blankly, especially Tish and Rebecca, as they hadn't been planning on going to the big dance and couldn't see what fun there would be to miss. It was weeks away, anyway – after half-term! But they wouldn't have dreamt of saying so right then.

'Er – like some birthday cake, Anestis?' asked Sue.

'Thank you, no.' He bowed low. 'I'm in a great rush now –' He gave Sue a beautiful smile. 'You girls must have it all.'

Mara went to see him off, still holding the dress.

'It's beautiful!' thought Rebecca once again.

Margaret Exton thought she would make Tish's life a misery.

'Poor you,' she said later, when she met her in the hall at Court House. 'Fancy having Robbie Anderson for an elder brother. Very sad.'

But Tish soon silenced her.

'You must know *just* how I feel,' she said sweetly. 'I wonder if he'll get himself expelled, like your elder sister did?'

The Fourth Year girl's bony face went rigid and she flounced off up the stairs to her room, flicking strands of long black hair away from her eyes. Last year Elizabeth Exton had been expelled from Trebizon – and it was partly Tish Anderson's doing that she'd been caught out.

'The fur is flying!' said Amanda Hancock, passing by.

'Maggie Exton walked straight into that,' said Moyra Milton.

Tish is in good form, thought Rebecca. *She's taking Robbie's behaviour right in her stride.*

In the kitchen that evening, with the rest of the six there, Tish said lightly:

'My brother's a big fool, that's all.'

'Oh Tish,' protested Sue, 'he's not that bad. He's never acted up like that before ...'

'He's never been *in love* before,' grumbled Tish. 'Here, give us some more cake!'

They all clamoured. 'Your diet, Elf!' Sue sighed, pushing one of the hands away, but then she relented. 'Oh, all right then! ... Here, Rebecca, you've left some of your icing behind.'

'The trouble is,' Tish went on, 'it's embarrassing having V. Slade in our house. It's going to be awful with Robbie hanging round here at weekends. Lovesick. Mean, moody –'

'And not a bit magnificent?' joked Sue.

'Exactly,' smiled Tish. Then she groaned. 'It's not funny. Why couldn't he have fallen for someone in Sterndale or Tavistock or – or –'

'Australia?' asked Rebecca.

'Perhaps he'll go off her soon?' suggested Elf helpfully.

'Not a hope,' said Tish, through a mouthful of cake.

'Well, then, maybe she'll go off *him*,' suggested Margot.

'That's more like it,' agreed Tish.

'Oh, poor Robbie!' said Mara suddenly. Her dark eyes were full of sympathy. 'That would be so sad for him.'

Tish just shrugged.

Next morning the big Assembly Hall swelled to the sound of four hundred girls singing the First Day hymn. Afterwards Miss Madeleine Welbeck, the principal, read out the notices from the platform. Rebecca and her friends were annoyed that Lady Edwina Burton had been made a prefect, but otherwise they approved.

Della Thomas had been elected Senior Prefect and Kate Hissup had stepped straight into her elder sister's shoes and would be Senior Head of Games. Pippa Fellowes-Walker, Rebecca's favourite prefect, was to be the new editor of the Trebizon Journal, but that had already been decided before Audrey Maxwell left in the summer.

A new school year had begun. Everybody had moved one rung up the ladder – except for poor Amanda Hancock who was staying down in the Fifth Year to retake all her exams. Rebecca & Co. were Third Years now.

All the form rooms were in old school. Although III Alpha's room was not as quaint as II Alpha's, which had been stuck almost in the rafters of the former manor house, it was very agreeable nevertheless and there were less stairs to climb. Their form mistress was Miss Hort, who was the middle school maths teacher. She was slightly mannish and very strict in the classroom but the girls who lived in Sterndale, where she was housemistress, said she had a great sense of humour and was just like a father to them.

Hockey trials took place and caused a lot of excitement. Third Year girls rarely got into senior teams, but Tish made the second eleven – and Joss leap-frogged straight into the first eleven, which was a record. She was also, of course, made Third Year head of games. Rebecca opted out of the trials and so did Sue. Sue's music was taking up more and more of her time. But she promised to play tennis with Rebecca sometimes – she was a good player, but had never been wholehearted about it.

Helena King, who was in Form III Beta and Norris House, was elected Magazine Officer and would thus decide all Third Year contributions for the school magazine. The six had wanted to elect Jenny Brook-Hayes again but they knew she was dying to get something into the Trebizon Journal herself and that she would be disqualified if she were Magazine Officer.

45

For Rebecca the most exciting part of the first ten days of term was playing singles on the staff tennis court. She couldn't beat Joss, of course, although it was exhilarating to play at such a pace. But she beat Sue both times they played and – to her own astonishment – she once beat Pippa Fellowes-Walker, who only last term had given up many hours to coaching her and nursing her along.

'You *have* come on!' exclaimed the Upper Sixth girl. 'Rebecca, you are going to leave me far *behind*.'

Rebecca looked forward to Exonford on the nineteenth, with a mixture of dread and high excitement.

Tish's fears that Robbie would come and hang round Court House were unfounded. The danger had apparently been nipped in the bud – by Virginia.

It was her exam year and it was common knowledge that she was going to have to work fantastically hard to pass.

'I've made a resolution, Robbie,' she told him, when he rang through to the coin box phone in Court House on the first Friday. Elf had the kitchen door open at the time and heard every word. 'I'm not going *anywhere* or doing *anything* on Saturdays, not even with you! I'll see you Sundays when I come over home. No, of course I haven't forgotten about the dance, that's months away, don't keep asking me! I'll be over tomorrow ... Why don't you do some work then? You've got exams, too, bad boy ... See you around tomorrow, then.'

These were golden September days for the friends. Miss Willis had decided that in view of the good weather sea-bathing and surfing could carry on. The first weekend Sue's brothers, David and Edward, came over on both afternoons from Garth College with a friend called Michael. They all had great fun surf-riding.

'Let's hope this weather holds, Rebecca!' said Harry, the school's lifeguard, on Sunday evening as he was waiting to lock up the white hut on the beach where the Malibu boards were kept.

'Let's hope so!' exclaimed Rebecca, gazing out to the breaker line. Margot was coming in, last of all, astride her rushing Malibu board in a cloud of spray, the salt water droplets shining on her black skin.

The vast beach was nearly empty now and the sun was going down over the sea, so that the water gleamed orange and silver. Rebecca could see a little fishing boat, a long way out. She suddenly thought of Robbie. He hadn't come anywhere near Trebizon, this weekend! It must be to do with that phone call Elf had overheard. If he couldn't see Virginia Slade he didn't want to see anyone. He was keeping his distance.

Rebecca didn't know whether to be sorry or pleased.

5
Invitations to the Dance

She badly wanted to know what her prospects were at tennis. She imagined that the truth would come in a blinding flash, when she started the training sessions at Exonford ... that she'd play plenty of hard tennis against the others in the squad. They'd been hand-picked, from all over the county – so she'd soon get to know whether she were any good or not!

That's what Rebecca thought but she was wrong.

Actually letting them play tennis was the last thing that David Driscoll had in mind. There were indoor tennis courts in the magnificent new sports centre at Exonford, as well as a gymnasium and a special practice wall with a mock tennis net. There were also some outdoor courts that they could use if the weather were fine. Each training session lasted for three hours. They spent one hour in the gymnasium, one hour at the practice wall and then – if they were lucky – the last hour on the courts. But even then they didn't play a proper game of tennis. They went through a gruelling form of training called 'Threes'.

A lot of the time in the gym the first day was spent on 'drill' – it was rather like being in an army squad – going through the basics, over and over again.

'One ... two ... three ... four ... five.'

'*One* ... take up your stance, feet correct. *Two* ... backswing. *Three* ... swing to make impact. *Four* ... angle your racket head to create spin. *Five* ... follow through!'

They drilled for the forehand, the backhand, the smash and the volley. There was a special drill for the service and they learnt that, too. They went through these drills, non-stop, standing in a line, tennis rackets in hand, not a tennis ball in sight. David Driscoll would shout out when anybody did anything wrong.

'Do this at home, too!' ordered the young coach. 'These are your fundamental strokes. They've got to be grooved right into your subconscious mind, with constant repetition. You've got to be able to produce them automatically, when you're on court, without ever having to stop and think!'

Next they moved on to the special practice wall. They repeated each stroke, and the drill that went with it, many times – using balls now. Again they worked in a long line and this time David Driscoll moved from pupil to pupil, correcting little faults as he went. 'Don't bend your arm, Rebecca –' 'John, your left foot's trailing.' 'Victoria, you haven't got your weight behind the ball, turn your shoulder!'

Finally they worked for an hour on the actual tennis courts. There were nine of them including the coach and they worked three to a court. Each pupil, for twenty minutes, had to face a barrage of shots from the other two, who were allowed to use the full width of the court. Retrieving ball after ball without pause (in fact doing the work of two players) was exhausting and hard, especially when David Driscoll was hitting. He changed in and out of each trio at regular intervals to speed up the pace. When Rebecca's turn came she almost ran herself into the ground, trying to get to every shot. 'Threes' was a very tough form of training.

But Rebecca knew that it was doing her tennis good. She knew it, as she showered afterwards, from the sense of achievement and the way her body ached.

All the members of the squad were beginning to realize something. There was much more to tennis than they'd ever imagined. If they were hoping to make good, it would be a long, hard road and they were only at the beginning of it.

'Some of you won't stick it,' David Driscoll told them calmly afterwards. They were sitting down to tea in the cafeteria at the sports centre. 'By Christmas some of you will have dropped out. But some of you will be ready to go on to the "D" squad. Just one or two.'

Rebecca's heart seemed to lurch inside her. Early on in the session, she'd realized something. They'd all played with David in a tournament, at least once. She wasn't the only one. In fact, because she'd been up in London, she'd been the last on his list.

She didn't know how she compared with the others in the squad – but David Driscoll did. He'd made it his business to get to know each one of them.

So the conversation they had later, when she was leaving to get the train back to Trebizon, gave her grounds for cautious optimism.

'I'm not going to be one of the ones who won't stick it out!' she informed him.

'I should hope not, Rebecca,' he replied. Then – 'You have one big asset for someone who wants to be a tennis player. You can run.'

The training sessions took place once a fortnight. In between Rebecca was expected to stick to a rigid programme of daily practice and she did so. The second session took place on October 3rd and David spent quite a lot of time on Rebecca's service. Afterwards, when she was leaving for her train again, he said casually :

'I came up by train today. Decided to leave my moped at home. If you can wait five minutes, we can travel back together.'

Rebecca was surprised. David Driscoll and his moped were usually inseparable.

Walking to the station together and then on the train, he opened out. It was strange to see him so talkative.

'This coaching doesn't give me enough to live on, I have to live off my mother. I haven't been able to get a job.' He seemed rather excited as he spoke. 'But a good job's come up at last! I'm on the short-list.'

'Oh, how nice,' said Rebecca, politely. It was embarrassing that someone so grown-up was suddenly confiding in *her*. 'What sort of job is it?'

'It's in work study!' he said. 'Based in London!' He looked quite animated. 'You have to spend a lot of time visiting factories. If I get it, I'll need a driving licence – I'm taking my test. I'd start after Christmas.' He looked regretful, just for a moment. 'Of course, I'd have to give up the coaching – but they'll easily get someone else for that.'

'I – I'm pleased for you,' Rebecca said awkwardly. 'I hope you get it.'

They parted company at Trebizon station, where Miss Willis was waiting with the school minibus to pick up Rebecca and three Sixth Formers who'd been to the Archaeological Museum in Exonford.

At the next session, around the middle of October, David Driscoll had once again left his moped behind. Once more Rebecca travelled back with him on the train. She was hoping she might seize the chance to ask him about her tennis – for she alternated between hope and despair – but he had other things on his mind.

'I got the job!' he exclaimed. 'I'll be giving up at Christmas. And I've passed my driving test.'

'Well, that's just – just terrific,' Rebecca said courteously. He seemed elated.

'If you knew how many jobs I've been after –! It's all right for these public school types, with all the right contacts, everything made easy –'

Rebecca looked startled.

'I don't mean you, Rebecca! You're ordinary somehow, just like me. I like you.'

Rebecca felt uncomfortable but he just carried straight on.

'Take the lot at Garth College. That boy Anderson's a prize example.' He suddenly smiled to himself, at some private joke, then checked the smile. 'Spoiled, half of them, born with a silver spoon –'

'Robbie Anderson's not like that!' exclaimed Rebecca. 'He works every holiday –'

'Oh, just for fun, I expect. He doesn't really need the money. But, okay, Rebecca – I know some of them are friends of yours. I won't hold it against you. You're alright!'

Rebecca felt hot with embarrassment and was relieved to see Trebizon station looming up. But there was more to come. As he helped her off the train, gripping her arm, he suddenly said:

'The next session's October 31st. You've got a big dance on at your place in the evening, haven't you?'

'I'm not going to that,' Rebecca said quickly, wishing he would let go of her arm.

'You mean nobody's asked you?' They were on the platform now. Then, very suddenly: 'Let me take you!'

Rebecca was startled. Then quickly she shook her head.

'Of course not! It's kind of you to suggest it. But I don't like dances! I'm not interested in that sort of thing!'

He released her arm and became very formal.

'Somebody's waving to you over there. Remember what I told you about your serve – keep working at it.'

'I will!' gasped Rebecca in relief. Mrs Barrington had come to collect her in the car and was standing by the ticket barrier, waving. 'I'd better dash now – 'Bye!'

As the housemistress drove her back to Trebizon, Rebecca felt rather miserable. *You mean nobody's asked you?* David Driscoll's words kept echoing through her mind. She could hardly admit it, even to herself, but his words had hit her on the raw.

But – go to the Hallowe'en Dance with David Driscoll? That would be ridiculous. It would be like going with a teacher.

It was Mara's dress that had started the rot.

One by one they had capitulated.

'Edward's asked me if he can take me to the dance,' Tish said rather shamefacedly, referring to Sue's brother.

53

'I think I might as well go – I hear the food's going to be marvellous.'

'And Michael's asked me,' admitted Sue. 'I might as well go. Why don't we ask Dave to take you, Rebecca, then we can all go!'

'No fear!' said Rebecca quickly. 'If your brother wanted to take me to the dance, he'd have asked me by now. Anyway, he's shorter than me.'

They begged and cajoled, but Rebecca wouldn't budge.

Then the list went up in the Court House common room. Girls who wanted partners for the dance were asked to put their names down. Mara persuaded her two roommates to sign up.

'Come on, Rebecca,' Margot said. 'You sign, too.'

'Be a sport,' said Elf. 'It won't be the same without you.'

But still Rebecca refused. As far as she was concerned, you only went to a dance with someone you really liked.

Some of the Fifth Years had got beautiful party dresses; almost as lovely as Mara's. Virginia Slade had tried hers on and paraded around the common room in it. It was blue and it made her blonde bubble curls look blonder than ever. She looked stunning.

For all Virginia's good resolutions, Rebecca noticed, she wasn't working that hard for her exams. At free times she often went off on her bicycle, in the kind of casual clothes that models wore. Sometimes she wore lipstick, which was forbidden.

She must be meeting Robbie Anderson down in the town. He hadn't been near Court House all term. Maybe he guessed how Tish felt about that, after all.

The weekend before the dance was half-term and Rebecca spent it at her grandmother's. If David Driscoll had touched her on the raw, her grandmother tore the wound wide open.

She had bought Rebecca a present.

'You need a proper dance dress at school now you're

getting older,' said old Mrs Mason with a twinkle in her eye. 'I got this outfit for you at the summer sales – it could have been made for you, Becky! You're to take it back to school with you. There's bound to be something special on at Christmas.'

It was a long dark green skirt with a pale green shirt and matching dark green waistcoat to go over it. Rebecca tried the outfit on and could have cried because it looked so beautiful.

As soon as she got back to school on the Monday evening, she hid the clothes under her mattress, before the others could see them.

When Rebecca went to Exonford on the afternoon of All Hallows Eve, she saw at once that David Driscoll had brought his moped. She felt relieved that he'd got tired of the idea of travelling by train.

'Pity you're not going to the dance tonight, Rebecca,' he said at tea-time. 'Somebody rather nice has agreed to let me take her. So I'd have seen you there.'

It was said rather meaningfully, but Rebecca didn't even notice.

She appeared cheerful that evening, helping the others to get ready for the dance. Mara looked lovely – so did Margot. Hooking Elf into her dress was a long job and a bit of a squeeze – but she looked really sweet in the end. *If only she'd stick to her diet for more than five minutes at a time!* thought Rebecca.

Sue looked very attractive although she refused to take her spectacles off. 'What – for Mike Brown?' she shrieked. 'He'd think I'd gone mad.'

Tish, who could look rather boyish with her short dark curly hair, looked very feminine tonight in her best red party dress. In fact, thought Rebecca, she looked beautiful.

When the escorts had arrived in their best suits and

they'd all gone to the dance, Court House suddenly seemed very silent and empty.

Rebecca's cheerfulness deserted her.

She had some books out on the homework table because she'd been planning to do some extra maths. Miss Hort had been terrifying her lately. But she couldn't settle to it. The windows were open on to the courtyard and in the far distance beyond the Hilary she could hear the strains of music coming from the big dining hall. She'd seen the hall earlier and hardly recognized it, alive with flickering Hallowe'en lanterns and streamers and huge silver witches that the seniors had made in the art room.

On impulse she went over to her bed and pulled her new party clothes out from their hiding place under the mattress. She lay them out on the bed and smoothed out the creases and just sat there, staring at them.

She didn't hear the footsteps in the hall.

There was a loud, urgent knock on the door.

'Who is it?' asked Rebecca, startled, bundling up the clothes. 'Come in.'

Somebody kicked the door open.

He stood there, out of breath because he'd been running. His unruly black curls had been plastered down with haircream and he wore a proper suit, with a waistcoat. He was holding a bunch of white carnations in his hand. He was tall and he was good-looking, just as Rebecca always pictured him.

'Come on, Rebeck. Get that track suit off and find a dress or something. I'm taking you to the dance.'

It was Robbie Anderson.

6

A Car Disappears

'Are those some party clothes you're holding now?' he
asked.

She'd leapt up, the outfit bundled up, trying to hide it
behind her back. The long silk tie that went with the shirt

was trailing down to the floor.

'Yes,' admitted Rebecca.

'Fine. Put 'em on, then. I'll go in the TV room and wait for you. Spurs are playing Arsenal. Here –' He thrust the bunch of carnations at her. 'Stick these in some water!' And then he was gone.

Rebecca rushed around at great speed, not quite sure why, except that Robbie made it seem the most natural thing in the world that she should hurry to change, and go to the dance with him, and that it wasn't up to her to argue! In any case, she didn't especially feel like arguing.

She filled a vase with water and arranged the flowers quickly. Then she hurtled through the kitchen into the laundry room, dragged out the ironing board and pressed her clothes at top speed. In the bathroom she just washed her hands and face – she'd had a hot shower before leaving the sports centre in Exonford – and then put on the long skirt and the pale green shirt and silk tie and the matching waistcoat. She brushed her long fair hair until it gleamed. Then she walked into the common room. Robbie at once leapt to his feet and switched off the TV set.

'Will I do?' she said.

He stared at her.

'You look ... You look good.'

They walked out of Court House and into the mild evening air. The trees were autumn colours now, but it was almost too dark to see them. As they took the shrub-lined path past the Barringtons' private forecourt, at the side of Court House, Robbie suddenly stopped.

'Hey – look!'

Just a few yards away, on the other side of the shrubs, the light from the Barringtons' front porch shone behind a parked car. It was a long, low graceful silhouette, just a flash of silver here and there where the light caught it.

'It's old Slade's car!' whispered Robbie, dragging Rebecca towards it. He ran his hands along the bonnet in silent worship. 'Don't you just love it?' he exclaimed.

'It – it's very nice,' said Rebecca politely. It had been parked there since the previous night. A lot of the girls had been admiring it. Margaret Exton had even sat inside it.

'But what's it doing here?' asked Robbie, suddenly puzzled. 'He's gone to Oxford for the weekend, some schoolmasters' conference.'

'Mr Barrington's gone to that as well – they've gone together. They went off in Barry's car last night.' Rebecca had seen them go. 'I know Mrs Barrington says that theirs is good on petrol.'

'Not half as much fun to drive though, I bet,' said Robbie, bending over and examining the instrument panel. 'Look at this – he's just dumped it here for the weekend and left the ignition keys in as well ... and he's my housemaster and he has the nerve to tell me *I'm* careless with my possessions!' Robbie laughed and touched the keys. 'Come on, Rebecca. I'd love to switch the engine on so you can listen – it's fantastically quiet ... it *purrs* ... it's the best new sports car that's been designed in Britain for about fifty years ...'

'Better not!' said Rebecca nervously, walking away. 'Come on.'

Robbie tore himself from the car and ran and caught up with her. 'It's made down here in the west country, you know.'

He took her arm because the path was full of potholes and they made for the brightly lit track that led to the main school buildings. As they drew nearer, the sound of music grew more distinct.

'Robbie,' blurted out Rebecca. 'Where's Virginia Slade?'

'At the dance.'

'I thought – Tish said ...'

'That was weeks ago. She's forgotten all about it. She's there with someone else. I saw them going over there together, just as our school bus turned into the car park.'

'David Driscoll?' asked Rebecca. Poor Robbie!

'Yes.' Robbie tried to sound casual. 'It's my own fault, I should have reminded her. She's got a memory like a sieve. That's one reason she's having to work twice as hard as anybody else for her exams. I haven't seen her for about a month. She hasn't even been coming over home on Sundays.'

Rebecca thought: *So it's David she's been seeing all this time – not Robbie! He doesn't seem to realize. Or does he?*

They cut round the side of Juniper House and entered the school quadrangle. Music throbbed loudly from the dining hall, underlaid by a babble of voices.

The music and laughter coming from inside, the flickering, grinning Hallowe'en lanterns at the windows, drew Rebecca on. She suddenly felt a great excitement. She was longing to go in! She quickened her pace as they crossed the big terrace towards the main doors, which were wide open. But Robbie suddenly pulled her back and stopped dead. His nerve almost failed him.

'I don't know whether I ought to go in or not,' he said.

Rebecca held her breath, waiting in suspense. Her first real dance! Was she going, or wasn't she?

'I wonder how well she knows Driscoll?' Robbie muttered then, under his breath. 'That's something I'd certainly like to know!'

The moment of indecision had passed.

With Rebecca tagging along behind, he marched resolutely into the dance.

Wild horses weren't going to keep him away.

Edward and Tish were sitting this one out, waiting for supper. There were tables all round the dance floor, each laid with cutlery for ten or a dozen people, candles guttering inside hollowed-out turnips. It was the last dance

60

before food was served. Earlier, Tish had found this corner table, well away from the band, where the whole crowd of them could be together and could hear themselves speak if they didn't want to dance. She was enjoying surveying the scene.

'Poor Elf, her partner's treading on her toes. The boy Margot's with doesn't look too bad. Oh, I wish Rebecca had come!'

'Robbie, too!' said Edward. He and Robbie were in the same boarding house at Garth College. 'D'you think he'll go off Virginia Slade now?'

'Not a chance!' said Tish.

'Think of the poor sap trudging back to school, with those flowers! I told him he was a fool to miss a party like this! I told him Rebecca had nobody to go with.'

'Not that nobody's asked her!' Tish said loyally. 'You'd be amazed if you knew who did! But she turned him down.'

'Well, spare me the gory details. I just told him that Rebecca was sitting over at Court twiddling her thumbs and why didn't he go and drag her out and forget all about V. Slade.'

'You *didn't*! Fancy wishing that on Rebecca!' said Tish scornfully. 'And as if he's going to forget about V. Slade. This'll make him crazier about her than ever.'

And then she froze.

'They're here,' she gasped. 'They've just arrived. Look at that outfit Rebeck's wearing – where did she get it? Oh, Edward, you *fool*.'

The music stopped and the dancers came off the floor. Sue and Mara and Co. saw Rebecca and Robbie and beseiged them, with cries of surprise, and dragged them over to the candlelit table in the corner.

'You're just in time for the food!'

'Rebecca, you've come after all – you look stunning!'

'You dark horse!'

'Hallo, Robbie!'

The next hour was great fun. The twelve of them sat squashed round the table, eating a delicious four course supper by candlelight, cracking jokes, fooling around, the band played a medley of the latest hit tunes the whole time that the meal was in progress. Virginia was far away – her party was sitting right at the opposite end of the hall. Rebecca caught a glimpse of her once through the semi-darkness, when somebody moved their head. Robbie didn't seem specially conscious of her.

But Tish seemed rather subdued.

'Sorry, Tish,' said Rebecca, when Robbie went of to seen if there were any more blackcurrant flan. 'I can see you think this isn't a good idea.'

'It's a rotten idea. He's just making use of you. And he's going to make himself miserable.'

'But I'm enjoying myself! I'm glad I've come!' Rebecca was disconcerted. 'He's just making the best of things, isn't he? He seems in quite a good mood.'

'It won't last,' Tish said darkly.

And it didn't.

After supper the dancing resumed and a great deal of intermingling went on. There was one awkward moment for Rebecca, when she walked straight into David Driscoll. In all the drama of being swept off to the dance by Robbie, she hadn't given it a thought that her tennis coach had offered to take her and she'd refused. After all, he was taking someone else now!

'Hallo, Rebecca. I thought you didn't like dances,' he said pointedly.

To Rebecca's surprise, there was quite an edge to his voice.

'I – I don't usually,' she said, in some confusion.

He became his usual, calm, courteous self again.

'Well, now you're here,' he smiled, 'I hope you're having

a good time. Keep working on those things I showed you this afternoon, won't you? I expect to see a big improvement in a fortnight's time.'

'Oh, yes!' said Rebecca, relieved that he'd changed the subject. 'I will, I promise.'

It was an embarrassing moment but it was the least of Rebecca's problems that evening. The greatest of Rebecca's problems was Robbie.

He'd meant so well. Having invited her to the dance, he fully intended to keep his temper under control. He was going to keep an eye on Virginia Slade and David Driscoll but at the same time see to it that Rebecca had a jolly good time. That's what he intended.

But it didn't work out that way.

As the evening grew late and the music more romantic, Virginia and David seemed inseparable. They danced together, time after time, and she gazed into his eyes with nothing short of adoration. She could hardly fail to be aware of Robbie's presence. For he kept dancing with Rebecca, right past her, eyes smouldering. But she never once looked at him or spoke to him. It was obvious that she either did not remember, or did not care, that she had once promised to let him take her to the dance.

Robbie's conversations with Rebecca sunk to the level of grunts and monosyllables. He was in a black mood and it was getting blacker all the time.

Tish could see exactly what was going on.

'Listen you two!' she said brightly, when they returned to the table after a waltz. 'We're all going down to the beach for a while, before the Garth bus goes back. We don't like this draggy music. Why don't you two come!'

'Too cold on the beach,' said Robbie. He was watching the dance floor. Virginia and David were still standing there, even though the music had stopped, waiting for the band to strike up again. She was brushing David's collar for him, with her hand. The band struck up again.

'Come on, Rebecca. Let's dance,' said Robbie.

So the others went down to the beach without them.

By now, Rebecca was longing for the evening to come to an end. What a drag!

At long last there came an announcement over the loud-speakers:

'The Garth College school bus leaves in five minutes. Will all boys who wish to travel on this bus please go round to the main school forecourt now. All good things come to an end, boys! I repeat, the Garth College bus is now leaving ...'

The hall had been thinning out for some time and now it thinned out still further as boys left to catch the bus and girls went with them to see them off. 'Come on, Robbie,' said Rebecca in relief. He was slumped at their table and seemed to be staring into space. 'You've got to get the bus now ...'

'I'm not getting the bus,' he grunted. 'I don't want to go yet. It's only three miles. I'll walk back to school – later.'

She realized that he was staring not into space but towards the glass doors that led out on to the terrace. David Driscoll was just taking Virginia through them. She had suggested they go out into the quadrangle gardens for some fresh air. Suddenly, Robbie stood up and pulled Rebecca to her feet.

'Come on. It's stuffy in here. Let's go outside where they're going.'

Rebecca had had enough.

'You can! I'm not! If you think Virginia needs a chaperone, then you go out there and chaperone her yourself!'

That was exactly what Robbie did think.

'I'm sorry, Rebeck,' he said, helplessly. 'But I'm worried about her. She's making a complete fool of herself, throwing herself at Driscoll.'

'I think you ought to go and catch the bus,' Rebecca said, more gently.

'No.' Robbie shook his head. He was in a miserable state. 'I'm going to stick around. But it's late – you're tired. Come on, I'm going to walk you back to Court House now.'

They walked back in silence. At the front door he patted her on the shoulder in an abstracted kind of way. 'Thanks, Rebecca.' She watched him walk away along the shrubbery path, heading back in the direction of the school. The haircream had long since ceased to have any effect and his dark curly hair was standing on end as usual. Her last impression was that he was in a wild state.

When Rebecca got to the room she switched on her bedside lamp took one of the white carnations out of the vase and smelt it and then lay down on the bed with it. She felt very, very tired. It had been a long and exhausting day.

When Sue and Tish came in they found that she had fallen fast asleep on top of the bed still wearing her party clothes, and clutching the carnation. They gently covered her up with some blankets and put her lamp out.

'I bet she's had a rotten time,' said Sue.

'I bet it's been a real drag,' said Tish.

Soon they were all fast asleep.

Nobody in Court House that night heard Mr Slade's new car being driven away from outside the Barringtons' front door. But, in the morning, it had disappeared.

7
Tennis Rivals

Rebecca did hear something during the night. It wasn't the sound of a car being driven away. It was an odd little noise.

It was after she'd woken up in the darkness, feeling

66

uncomfortable and wondering why her pyjamas felt hot and why the sheets felt rough. Then she realized that she'd fallen asleep fully dressed and wasn't between the sheets, anyway. She groped in the darkness for her bedside lamp and switched it on and then blearily looked at her watch. It was exactly three o'clock in the morning!

Still half asleep, she undressed and got into her pyjamas and flung her party outfit to the floor. She'd fold it up in the morning. Right now she was just aching to get back to sleep!

It was then that she heard the noise, coming from somewhere outside in the courtyard. *Squeak – whirrr – squeak ... squeak – whirrr – squeak ... squeak – whirrr – squeak ...* It was an eerie little sound. What was it – a bird – a bat? Rebecca shivered and switched off her lamp. *Squeak – whirrr – squeak ...* there was the noise again. A trailing creeper rattled against the window. It was strange to think that while they all slept, out there in the darkness the night had a life of its own. For a moment she felt scared. Then she listened to the sound of Tish and Sue's regular breathing coming from the other beds and felt comforted.

She soon went back to sleep again.

'Wake up, Rebeck! Here's a cup of tea!'

It was morning and that was Tish's voice. She and Sue were both up and dressed, in denim jeans and checked shirts, bringing her a cup of tea in bed. They both looked very cheerful.

'Swallow it down and get dressed!' said Sue.

'We'll give you some "Threes" after breakfast, over on the staff tennis court!'

'Will you?' Rebecca sat up and rubbed her eyes, feeling pleased. 'Will you really?'

David Driscoll had told all the members of the squad to play 'Threes' as often as possible, in between training sessions, because it was such good practice. Tish and Sue obliged as often as they could – except that on Sunday mornings they usually liked to laze around.

After an hour's hard tennis practice, Rebecca felt really good again. Tish and Sue wanted her to forget all about the dance and she did. What marvellous friends they were! It was also going to be a beautiful day, surprising for the beginning of November.

'You're getting fantastically good,' said Sue, as they walked back to Court House afterwards. 'The way you get some of those balls back – you're like a gymnast!'

'Bet you'll win your games next Saturday,' said Tish.

'I hope so,' sighed Rebecca. 'It's all going to help decide who goes in the D squad after Christmas! We'll only play if the weather's fine.'

As part of the winter training programme David Driscoll had now arranged a series of friendly matches for the juniors during November, at times when they didn't go to Exonford. The following Saturday the four girls in the squad were to play against Caxton High School, who kept some tennis nets up during the winter. They would then have to report their scores at the next training session.

'Well, it's going to be fine today all right,' said Tish, gazing up at the blue sky in surprise. 'D'you think Mrs Barrington will let us go in the sea this afternoon?'

'Doubtful,' said Sue gloomily.

Surfing and sea-bathing had officially ended at half-term.

'Hey!' said Rebecca. She pointed her tennis racket as Court House came in sight. 'Look – a police car!'

They rushed back to the boarding house. There was a crush in the hall and girls were hanging over the banisters, all agog. A police officer was moving around, asking questions and taking notes.

'What's going on?' mouthed Tish.

'It's that flash car that was parked here!' whispered Elf.

'Mr Slade's?' asked Rebecca quickly. 'What about it?'

'It's gone!' said Margot. 'Somebody pinched it during the night! Mrs B found it gone when she looked outside this morning –'

'She rang the police straight away!' finished Mara.

Virginia Slade was talking to the police officer in a shrill voice and looking agitated.

'It can't have been any of the boys who were at the dance, sir!' she was saying. 'Daddy's car was still there very late – I saw it when I came in. The college boys had all gone by then! Besides they wouldn't – they just wouldn't – Daddy's a housemaster there and they all *like* him ...'

'Could be one of 'em has a grudge against him,' said the policeman. 'Or just high spirits after the dance. The car'll be most likely found within a few hours. They usually are, once our lads get on the job.'

Tish and Rebecca looked at one another, uneasily.

'On the other hand it might be nothing to do with the dance at all,' the officer said stolidly. 'There's been a spate of joy-riding this year. There was a lot of it when the holiday-makers were down in the summer.' Rebecca felt a slight sense of relief. 'Of course, it's a bit late for tourists. But there's a few boys in the town I wouldn't trust an inch ...'

'I'm sure you'll find it's one of them,' Virginia insisted. 'I was the last person around last night, and the car was still here.'

'Er – about what time would that be, miss?'

Some of the Fifth Years grinned and looked at each other. It was an open secret what time Virginia crept upstairs.

'Midnight,' she said, looking embarrassed.

'Dead on!' said Amanda Hancock. 'I heard the clock strike.'

Dutifully the officer wrote it down and shut his note-book.

'Taken some time after midnight,' he muttered. He'd found out enough for the present and was edging towards the front door. 'Right, I'll just have another word with Mrs Barrington. We'll soon find the car.'

'Do you think you'll find it by tea-time?' Virginia pleaded. 'That's when Daddy's due back from Oxford. It'll be a terrible shock for him.'

The officer grunted. He'd already discovered from several of the girls that the ignition keys had been left in the car.

'Careless of him to leave the keys in, then,' he said.

But Virginia looked so pretty and appealing that he immediately softened his attitude a little.

'I suppose he thought it would be safe enough, tucked away up here. Careless, all the same. Don't worry, miss, with luck we'll have recovered the car by the time your father gets back.'

The officer left and the girls dispersed in all directions. The six friends went into the kitchen and made tea with tea-bags and talked non-stop about the drama. But Tish and Rebecca were rather subdued. They had looked at each other once, but somehow they didn't dare look at each other again.

Rebecca spent most of Sunday playing singles, first with Pippa in the morning and then all afternoon with Joss Vining, who was in superb form. When Joss had gone and Rebecca was letting down the net, her friends came rushing over to the tennis court.

'We can swim in the sea!' Tish said excitedly. 'Just for half an hour. Mrs Barrington's been down there to look, it's as warm as anything and not at all rough. Come on, Rebeck!'

'Yippee!' said Rebecca. She felt hot and sticky all over.

She rushed back to the boarding house to get her swimming things and grabbed her watch, which she very rarely wore, so that they could keep an eye on the time. Then all of them except Mara raced down to the beach and changed in the school beach huts.

It was a wonderful swim, cool and sweetly refreshing, with the sun just starting to go down. Rebecca enjoyed it very much.

Afterwards she and Tish changed in the extra large hut at the end. It was the first time they'd really been alone that day. Suddenly there was no avoiding the subject any longer.

'Robbie was awful last night, wasn't he,' said Tish.

'Terrible,' said Rebecca.

'It wasn't much fun for you. When did he leave? He didn't get on the bus with the other boys.'

'He decided to walk back,' said Rebecca. 'I don't know what time he left. He saw me back to Court and then went back to the dance. He was in a very funny mood.'

'I expect he left very late. Maybe kept watch on them, until David had gone home. And that was midnight. Wonder what he did after that?'

Rebecca could tell she was worried.

'You think he might have taken the car, don't you, Tish?'

But Robbie phoned Rebecca that evening. It was the first phone call she'd ever received at Court House.

'Hi,' he said. 'I want to apologize.' He wasn't finding it easy. 'About last night. I behaved stupidly. After dragging you to the dance in the first place, I wanted you to have a good time. And I spoiled everything. I'm sorry, Rebeck.'

'That's all right, Robbie,' said Rebecca. The cloud that had been lurking around all day was beginning to move away. 'Forget it.'

'Have the police found old Slade's car, yet?' he asked. The news, it seemed, had travelled fast.

'No,' said Rebecca. 'He got back from Oxford at tea-time and they went straight down to the police station in Barry's car. But it hadn't turned up then.'

'I hope it's okay when it *is* found,' said Robbie, with some feeling. 'I hope the stupid blighters haven't damaged it.'

'Let's hope not.'

Rebecca suddenly felt positively happy.

After putting the phone down she went straight to find Tish. Whatever had she and Tish been worrying about?

The friendly match against Caxton High School the following Saturday was Rebecca's first real test. Unlike the mixed doubles at Trebizon when David Driscoll had been her partner, and she'd had very little to do, she was playing singles this time. She was on her own.

Only the girls in the squad played – the boys were playing somewhere else – and their opponents were four Sixth Form girls at Caxton High, all of them in their school tennis team.

Everything came together in Rebecca's game that day.

She won both her singles matches. 7–5, 6–4 and 7–5, 7–6.

Victoria and Lucy-Ann lost both their matches.

The fourth girl in the squad, Madeleine Marks, won both times, just like Rebecca. And her scores were almost identical.

At the last training session, on the day of the dance, David Driscoll had told them that there would be one vacant place for a girl in the D squad after Christmas – but no more.

It was beginning to look as though Rebecca and Madeleine might be rivals for that place.

Rebecca had the kind of mind that stored up useless bits of information. She'd read somewhere that the British police force recovered 99 per cent of all stolen cars. That within hours of a car being hi-jacked, police patrol cars throughout Britain were armed with its registration number and a full description.

Ninety-nine per cent were recovered – and usually within 48 hours.

On the other hand, if they weren't recovered within 48 hours, they were usually not recovered at all.

John Slade's car was not recovered within 48 hours. It had still not been recovered two weeks later, when Rebecca went for her next training session at the Exonford sports centre.

It was the most splendid car. But it looked as though it were one of the elusive 1 per cent that just seem to vanish from the face of the earth.

8

A Dramatic Telephone Call

Something else had disappeared. Rebecca's watch. It was a nuisance because without it she nearly missed the train to Exonford on that second Saturday in November.

'I *wonder* where I left it?' she frowned to herself, as

she watched the fields and hedges rushing by. 'It *must* have been at the sports centre, last time I was there.'

Rebecca didn't like wearing a watch, so only wore one when she really needed to. She usually left it lying around in their study bedroom. She had been vaguely conscious that she'd mislaid it for about a fortnight now, and had looked for it once or twice. Finally, because she always liked to wear it to Exonford, she ransacked the room on Friday and even asked Mrs Devenshire, the school secretary, about it. But no-one had found it.

It looked as though she *must* have left it at the sports centre, except she could have sworn that she was wearing it when she came away from there on the afternoon of the Hallowe'en Dance ...

Training went remarkably well for Rebecca that day. She spent a lot of time on court, serving again and again under David Driscoll's watchful eye. Only twice did she serve a double fault.

'You've really got it, Rebecca!' he said. For once, he showed some feeling. 'Tremendous!'

Afterwards, in the cafeteria, he gathered them all round him.

'Next Saturday, weather permitting, there's the friendly at King's Club in Clifford. Remember to write all your scores down on your record sheets. If it rains, it'll be called off. The big one is here, in a fortnight's time – the Exonford Indoor Junior Tournament. You're all entered. No training that day, of course.

'I spoke to Mrs Seabrook on the phone this morning. It's definite. Two players are leaving D squad after Christmas, one boy and one girl. That means two of you will be moving up. We know the boy's going to be Toby –'

He paused as they all cheered Toby and clapped him on the back, though it had been obvious for some weeks that the lanky fourteen-year old was bound to be promoted.

'It's not so easy to decide who the girl will be. Except

it'll be either Rebecca or Madeleine. I'll make my recommendations to the county officials after the Indoor Tournament. After that, there's one more training session before the Christmas break, then I'll be leaving county tennis. You'll have a new coach in January.'

Rebecca and Madeleine looked at each other. It was between the two of them! Definitely.

Rebecca's mind was in a turmoil when she left the sports centre and hurried to catch her train. It was in such a turmoil that she completely forgot to enquire about her lost watch! *Oh, dash it,* she thought, as the train went out. *Now I'll have to wait another fortnight.*

But she had much more important things on her mind. Once it had been only a day dream – getting promoted to the county D squad after Christmas – now it was really within her grasp!

She had to play well at the King's Club next Saturday.

Then would come the Indoor Junior Tournament at Exonford. It would be played in a proper competition atmosphere. David would be certain to fix the draw so that Rebecca had to play against Madeleine. Whatever happened, she had to beat her!

The November skies were grey the following Saturday, but the rain held off and the friendly tournament took place at King's Club. Rebecca did very well indeed – rather better than Madeleine. She arrived back at Court House on Saturday evening feeling on top of the world.

'How did it go, Rebeck?' Tish asked eagerly.

'Fine! Lost one set and won three! How about the hockey match?'

'We won 3–2 and I scored!'

They grabbed hands and twisted round and round in the hall, exuberantly. Then suddenly Sue burst in through the front door, holding her violin case and looking full of news. Moyra Milton was just behind her, with her clarinet.

The two girls had been in the Barringtons' part of Court House. This often happened on Saturdays. Mr Barrington would invite all the Music Scholars round for tea and some informal music making in his own home – Sue enjoyed these sessions very much.

'Guess what!' cried Sue.

'What?'

'Mr Slade's car has been found! He rang up Barry just now –'

'It *hasn't*!'

'Where – where?'

Their voices were loud and girls started to appear from all directions – out of the common room –out of the kitchen – down the stairs, all asking questions!

'What happened?'

'Tell us!'

'It was near Trebizon all the time! Only three miles away! Hidden in the funniest place –'

'The British police are wonderful, yes?' grinned Aba, coming from her room round the corner. Aba was a brilliant runner and shared with Ann and Anne – so the friends called it the Three A's Room. 'They found the car?'

'They've taken their time!' said Rebecca. 'I read somewhere –'

'No, not the police!' exclaimed Sue. 'They'd more or less given up –'

'It was some old farmer called Bond who found it!' butted in Moyra Milton. 'He's got that big farm, up on the Clifford road. He found it hidden in one of his barns!'

'He *didn't*!' Everyone was amazed, gathering round.

'He did!' Sue took up the story. 'It's a barn full of hay bales. He wouldn't normally have gone in there until after Christmas – till the winter gets hard. But one of his sheep escaped and got in amongst the hay bales. And, you'll never guess, the car was right in the middle of the hay! The person who pinched the car had moved a whole stack of bales to put it there, and then stacked them all back up again and put some over the top, so the car was *completely* hidden!'

'The poor chap nearly dropped dead with shock to see a car like that hidden in the middle of all his winter feed!' laughed Moyra.

'Is the car all right?' Rebecca wanted to know.

'It's been crashed – the wing's all bashed in,' said Sue. 'But perfectly driveable. It looks as though the thief hit a tree or something up on the Clifford road and then drove it across a couple of fields to get it to the barn and hide it. All in the middle of the night presumably.'

'What a peculiar business,' said Elf. 'They usually just dump them! But thank goodness it's been found! I wonder how much the damage will cost?'

'I wonder who took it?' mused Tish.

'They'll never catch them now!' said Margaret Exton scornfully. She'd been listening from the top of the first flight of stairs.

'I should think Mr Slade's only too relieved to get the car back,' said Moyra. 'I should think that's the end of the story.'

But Moyra was wrong. It wasn't the end of the story.

Robbie Anderson telephoned Court House half-an-hour later and asked to speak to Rebecca. Anxiously wondering what he had to say, she went and took the call at the coin-box phone by the stairs.

'Rebecca!' He sounded rather distressed. 'Slade got his car back this afternoon. You should see it! A beautiful car like that and it looks a real mess!'

'It's only a car!' said Rebecca, startled. She was on the verge of nervous laughter. Robbie sounded so emotional about it, almost as though the car were alive and had been injured and disfigured for life! 'He'll get it fixed.'

'I've got to find out who took it!' said Robbie. 'I want

78

to know if you saw or heard anything that night – ask Tish – ask everybody –'

'We have an Action Committee sometimes,' said Rebecca, humouring him, 'and we're quite good at solving mysteries, us six. But I don't think we're going to be able to solve this one –'

'You don't understand! *It's not funny.* Slade thinks *I* did it.'

'You?' Rebecca's smile vanished.

'Yes, me. Look, I know it's pretty hopeless, but you lot try and find out anything suspicious that happened that night – anything at all. Will you, Rebeck?'

'Yes. But – but Robbie –'

'Yes?'

'Why have you rung me and not – well, not Tish?'

'She mightn't believe I didn't do it. Sisters can be pretty horrible at times. Try and convince everybody, won't you?'

Rebecca found Tish and the others in the common room and told them.

Tish at once look grimly worried.

'I don't like the sound of it,' she said, just as Robbie had predicted she would. 'Mr Slade must have something to go on –'

'Of course Daddy's got something to go on!' exclaimed a voice from the doorway.

They all looked round. Virginia Slade stood there, angry, high colour in her cheeks. She'd just got back from Garth College where she'd been helping her mother with teas for a house rugby match.

'What?' asked Rebecca coldly. 'What's he got to go on?'

'For one thing, Robbie Anderson was hanging around after the dance, I saw him –'

'Oh, it's Robbie *Anderson* now, is it?' snapped Tish, getting edgy.

79

'For another,' said Virginia, ignoring her, 'he didn't get back to College until two in the morning, because a prefect caught him coming in and it's in the detention book –'

'So what!' said Rebecca. 'He had to walk back after the dance!'

'Three miles?' said Virginia. 'The dance finished at eleven! Anyway, even if you ignore all that, Daddy's found his handkerchief in the car! It's got his name tape on it – R. J. Anderson. So that's that!'

Tish groaned. So did Sue. Margot and Mara and Elf just kept quiet. Rebecca caught her breath. Robbie's handkerchief, found in the car! He hadn't even bothered to mention it.

'Oh, the fool!' Tish groaned again and covered her face with her hands.

'He hasn't even got the courage to own up!' said Virginia scornfully. He doesn't know how lucky he is! Daddy's notified the police that the car's turned up, but he hasn't told them anything about Robbie! He likes Robbie. He'll punish him, of course, and your parents will have to foot the bill, but he won't hand him over to the police. All he's asking Robbie to do is to have the guts to own up and say he's sorry and Robbie won't!'

'Maybe he can't,' said Rebecca. 'Maybe he didn't do it.'

'Of course he did it! He's just a raving idiot!' exclaimed Virginia. 'To think I liked him once!'

That was too much for Tish. She leapt to her feet.

'Don't you be so clever!'

'How dare you –' began Virginia.

'You're partly to blame for all this!' yelled Tish. 'You promised Robbie he could take you to the dance and he turned up in his best suit and he even bought you some flowers – he's crazy about you! He went wild when he saw you at the dance with David Driscoll. He tried to stop himself but he was just in the mood to do something wild and stupid –'

She stopped. Virginia looked stunned.

'Did – did I promise he could take me to the dance?' She ran a hand down her cheek. 'Is that why he was behaving so strangely?' Her lower lip started to tremble slightly. 'Yes, yes. I did promise him. I remember now. I'd no idea it mattered that much –'

She turned and hurried from the room, looking very upset.

Some girls out in the hall who'd been listening, quickly dispersed. Margaret Exton was amongst them. She was quite enjoying this little drama over Robbie Anderson and the car.

Later that evening, when everybody was getting ready for bed, Rebecca went through to the kitchen to get a drink and she heard Virginia's voice in the hall. She was speaking very softly into the phone.

'Look, Robbie ... was it revenge, or something ... was that it? I'm sorry ... I behaved horribly ... I'll take some of the blame with Daddy. But please own up –'

There was the distinct sound of a click at the other end.

'Robbie – listen –'

He's hung up on her! thought Rebecca. *He didn't take the car and she doesn't believe him and he's furious! But what's going to happen next?*

9
The Six Investigate

What happened next was that Robbie smashed the Head's window and got himself thrown out of College.

'Doctor Simpson's suspended him till the end of term!' panted Edward Murdoch. Sue's brother was almost choking for breath as he cycled into the courtyard. 'If you want to see him off he's catching the 12.30 train to London!'

It was Sunday mid-morning. The six friends were sitting on the low wall in the courtyard and they'd been endlessly discussing the question of Robbie and the car. Rebecca had told them about Virginia's phone call and it was gradually beginning to dawn on them all, even Tish, that Robbie was behaving like someone who was not guilty, but innocent.

Then Edward appeared, rather pale and staring-eyed after cycling his hardest from Garth College to Trebizon.

'You mean, your Headmaster's decided that Robbie's guilty?' asked Sue, shocked. 'Just like that?'

Tish and Rebecca were simply stunned.

'No,' said Edward.

'What happened then?'

'Robbie smashed a window in the Head's study. Just chucked a paperweight clean through it. Slade took him over there, first thing this morning. It was like a tribunal, Robbie said. Motson was there, he's the house prefect, with the detention book, showing how late he got in after the dance. Slade had the handkerchief. They were all getting at him, Doctor Simpson was trying to get him to confess and – well – he just completely lost his cool and picked up the paperweight and chucked it through the window and walked out.'

'Phew!' said Tish. She was beginning to recover from the shock. 'And he's only been suspended – not expelled?'

'The Head's told him to go home and think things over. To think very hard about whether he took the car that night or not. That even if he's innocent he's not allowed to go around smashing windows and he'll decide later whether he can be reinstated at College next term or not. In the meantime – the Head says – he's going to try and make some enquiries of his own.'

'Good for him!' exclaimed Rebecca.

'Then he's not convinced?' said Sue eagerly. 'He's not convinced that Robbie pinched the car and smashed it up?'

'He just doesn't know *what* to think,' said Edward.

'Of course Robbie did not take the car,' said Mara softly. 'What does he say about that handkerchief, please Edward?'

'He says he's often sat in the car,' shrugged Edward. 'Secretly, when old Slade's not been around. Just getting the feel of the gear lever ... dusting the instrument panel with his handkerchief ... holding the steering wheel ...'

'That's it!' Tish almost shrieked the words. 'I can just see him doing it!' A look of utmost relief crossed her face. 'I'm convinced!'

'About time,' said Rebecca.

'I've got to run now!' said Edward, picking up his bike. 'I dodged away from rugby practice – I just had to come and see you – but I'd better get back fast. Try and get to the station and see Robbie! Hurry – there isn't much time – let him know you're behind him!'

Rebecca ran all the way to Parkinson, the Upper Sixth boarding house. Pippa had her own car now and she kept it at school. There it was – the big blue Renault – but would she be around to drive it! She was – and, as usual, Rebecca's favourite prefect didn't ask any awkward prying questions but just drove the six of them, all squashed together, down to the mainline station at Trebizon.

'We're in plenty of time!' exclaimed Tish. She looked all round the station. 'Robbie isn't here yet. He'll have his trunk and everything. I expect he'll come by taxi.'

She was very matter-of-fact about it, though the thought of poor Robbie with his trunk packed sent a twinge through Rebecca.

They sat around the station and soberly made plans. Pippa had gone into the town to find a Sunday newspaper and would come back for them later. They kept watching

84

the station forecourt, expecting Robbie to arrive at any moment.

'Looks like the Action Committee's alive and kicking again,' said Elf.

'We ought to have a banner and some flags!' said Tish, a wild light in her eyes. She was joking, and yet serious. '*The Six Support You!*'

'He'll be pleased we're here,' said Rebecca. 'But what are we going to say ... ? We've got to think about that!'

'We can promise faithfully to try and do what he asked you last night!' said Sue. 'Ask questions – try and find out who really pinched the car!'

'Detective work!' agreed Tish. 'Like that missing cash box!' she added, remembering a former triumph. Then she became subdued. 'Only this is ten times worse. D'you realize this is Robbie's big exam year? Daddy's going to turn grey.'

'We can promise Robbie, can't we?' said Margot. 'We can at least promise to try.'

But Robbie never turned up.

The 12.30 train to London came in – and went out – without him.

'Edward must have told us the wrong train,' said Sue in disgust. 'Trust him to get it wrong. It's the only explanation.'

They were sitting having Sunday lunch in the school dining hall. They were all at the same table this year, with Joss Vining head of table. They'd wanted to keep watch at the station but Pippa wouldn't hear of it. They were expected back at school for lunch. It was roast beef and Yorkshire pudding – delicious – and probably worth coming back for, Rebecca decided.

'It's not a disaster,' said Tish, who'd really been very hungry. 'I'll phone home late this evening, when Robbie's back. Tell him how we all feel – how we're going to try our best to find out things.'

'And we might as well start investigating this afternoon!' said Elf, through a mouthful of peas. 'Lessons start again tomorrow.'

With the Exonford Indoor Tournament coming up on Saturday, Rebecca badly needed her Sunday tennis practice. But she put it aside.

Between them, they spoke to every single girl in Court House – and there were thirty-six of them – to ask if they'd heard or seen anything peculiar, anything at all, some time after midnight on the night of the Hallowe'en Dance. The only exception was Virginia Slade. They didn't ask her.

They even explored every inch of the Barringtons' private forecourt, where the car had been parked that weekend, in case there was the smallest clue.

'Aren't they pathetic?' sneered Margaret Exton.

Later, she said to Tish:

'He made it then? He got himself thrown out. You wondered if he would – remember?'

Tish pushed past her, furiously, and went to the telephone. It was eight o'clock. Even allowing for a later train, and a long journey, Robbie should be home by now. She picked up the telephone and dialled the operator, feeling very keyed up, and asked to reverse the charges.

'Tish?' That was her elder sister's voice. She sounded worried.

'Helen! Of course!' Suddenly Tish remembered. Her parents were in America for two weeks. When they went on these trips her sister always came home to look after the house and feed the animals. 'Is Robbie there?'

'No.'

So he was still on his way!

'Helen, d'you know what's happened –?' began Tish.

'You bet I do. The school rang here this morning and told me to expect him. They'll be writing to Mummy and

Daddy this week. What a lovely surprise for them when they get back from the States next Sunday!'

'Helen, Robbie didn't pinch that car and we're going to try and prove it. Don't be horrible to him when he gets in. Can you ask him to ring here, if it's before nine o'clock?'

'As a matter of fact I can't,' said Helen, 'because he isn't coming home until next Sunday.'

'*What?*' said Tish.

'He phoned me this afternoon. He said there was no point in coming home yet, till Mummy and Daddy get back, and he's shacking up with some pal of his in London for a few days.'

'Who's that?' asked Tish. 'Got their phone number?'

'No,' said Helen. 'Didn't ask for it. I haven't the faintest desire to speak to Robbie. What a menace! Going around smashing windows! It's going to be bad enough when he does get home. What an almighty row there's going to be!'

'So there's no way I can contact him?'

'Sorry, Tish. I suppose I should have asked him who these people are in London – but it was all a bit rushed. What's this you're saying about someone pinching a car? I expect he'll ring through again in the next couple of days. I'll tell him to contact you, okay?'

The six felt rather glum after that. It was such a let-down, somehow, not being able to let Robbie know how they felt.

'But we just press on regardless,' said Tish, lying in bed that night.

'We've drawn a complete blank today,' said Rebecca, sadly. It had been rather boring, asking girls the same questions over and over again and being laughed at by some for presuming to be 'detectives'. 'We'll have to think what to do next.'

'One thing we ought to do is get a good look in Margaret Exton's room,' said Tish, darkly. 'I saw her sitting in Mr Slade's car that weekend!'

'Well, Robbie made quite a habit of that. So what!' said Sue.

'It's a funny thing for a girl to do,' said Tish. 'I've been thinking about it.' She yawned. 'We might find something in her room. You never know.'

What? wondered Rebecca. A spare wheeel? A set of spanners? In the darkness she moved her head on the pillow and smiled. None of them liked Margaret Exton, but, really, this was ridiculous. Tish was going off her head!

'You can search her room!' she said. 'Blowed if I'm going to!'

'Nor me!' said Sue.

Tish searched Margaret Exton's room, which was on the first floor of the boarding house, during Monday dinner hour. She found the others just as they were walking over to the science block for biology and her face was blazing with triumph.

'She's got a car manual under her pillow!' she whispered. 'And it's for the Masters X 19 – that's Mr Slade's car!'

It seemed like incredible news – astonishing.

But when Sue went to orchestra practice, after biology, she had a long chat with Moyra Milton. Moyra didn't like Margaret Exton, but she knew her quite well. She had the room next door to her in Court and they were both in form IV Alpha – and she knew all about the car manual.

'Bad luck, Tish,' said Sue, at tea-time. 'Freddie Exton's just taken over Masters!' Margaret Exton's father was a well-known business tycoon. 'He's promised to give her a Masters X 19 for her sixteenth birthday, so naturally she's interested in it!'

Tish felt deflated.

'She won't be able to get a licence at sixteen,' she said stubbornly.

'She'll just drive it round the grounds at home. They've got an enormous place in Surrey. Oh, Tish, I think that's all there is to it.'

'She's kept pretty quiet about it, hasn't she?' mused Margot.

'You're right!' said Tish. Her mind was working hard and her interest was beginning to revive. 'You'd think she'd have been boasting about it. But she hasn't! Hey – if you were Margaret Exton and you knew you were going to get a car just like Slade's for your sixteenth birthday, wouldn't you just be dying to try it out –?'

'Possible,' agreed Rebecca. 'But only just. I mean surely her father will let her try one out at home, anytime she wants ...'

'She couldn't wait!' exclaimed Elf. 'That was it!'

They were all getting excited now – except for Rebecca.

'We may have solved it!'

'Good old Tish!'

'But how do we prove it?'

'I've got an idea,' said Tish. 'It's half day Wednesday. Let's trace the exact route the car took that night – go to the barn where it was found – see if there's *anything* that could be evidence ...'

'I've got a faint feeling,' said Rebecca, frowning, 'that I saw Margaret Exton going upstairs in her dressing gown, when I came back from the dance.'

But nobody was listening. Nobody wanted to know about that.

'Even if you did, she could have sneaked out after midnight. She doesn't even share a room with anybody. There'd be nobody to hear her leave or come back! That's why we've got to find proof some other way.'

'Okay,' said Rebecca. 'We'll go to the barn.'

She'd been planning on spending the whole of Wednesday afternoon playing tennis. Instead, the six of them set off on borrowed bicycles and headed up towards the Clifford Road. It was a long, straight, wide road that ran through farmland. For the mile approaching Bond's farm it ran downhill and Rebecca enjoyed the sensation of cycling fast. Her fair hair flew out behind her. The rushing air went up her sleeves and under her armpits. Her eyes watered a little. It turned into an exhilarating race between her and Margot and Tish, with Rebecca sprinting into the lead, Margot overtaking and Tish finally winning the day with sheer leg muscle.

'What a place for a burn-up!' panted Margot, as they drew up, near a farm gate. There was a lone farmhouse in the distance, set well back from the road. 'Just like a race track, hey?'

'The joy-rider must have had a fantastic time,' said Rebecca. 'Until they hit the tree or something!'

'That could be the very tree,' said Sue, pointing ahead as she came up beside them.

There was a solitary young tree ahead. It grew right on the edge of the road, just where it suddenly narrowed. Waiting for Mara and Elf, who were puffing along some way back, they went and examined it. Sure enough, the bark showed signs of damage.

'I can just picture it,' said Rebecca, shutting her eyes, 'belting along in the moonlight, faster and faster, brooommph! Then something coming from the Clifford direction, road narrows ... brake ... swerve ... scrape into the tree!'

'And there's the barn, must be!' said Tish, pointing across the fields. 'From the gate back there a track leads straight to it!'

But they didn't find anything in the barn, except for one – rather obvious – clue.

'Here, Tish,' said Sue, straining and heaving, 'feel the weight of this hay bale a minute!'

'Well?' Tish obliged. 'They always weigh heavy!'

Rebecca at once lifted one up herself, and then tried to

lift it to shoulder height. Phew! She let it drop. Of course! *That* was why it couldn't be Margaret Exton.

'Imagine unstacking all these bales, to get the car in!' said Sue. 'And then building a high wall of them round the car afterwards, to hide it!'

'A girl could never do it!' said Rebecca.

Tish looked crestfallen, so did the other three.

At bedtime that night, Rebecca felt pretty dejected herself. They were no nearer solving the mystery. But in the meantime, she'd lost a lot of tennis practice this week – and it was the tournament on Saturday! The day when she had to prove she was better than Madeleine Marks.

She *must* get some practice in tomorrow!

'Got it!' said Tish suddenly, just as she was climbing into bed. 'Isn't it obvious? Margaret Exton must have had somebody with her! Who did she go to the dance with?'

'She didn't,' said Sue.

Sometimes Tish could be as stubborn as a mule!

Thud ... thwack ... forehand ... backhand ... drive ... smash! Afternoon school had finished on Thursday and Rebecca was belting the ball against the wall of Norris House as hard as she could, non-stop. She'd no idea how long she'd been going – was it tea-time yet? Where was that dratted watch of hers, anyway?

Phew! She wouldn't mind a swim!

Watch! Swim!

Rebecca suddenly stopped in her tracks and caught the tennis ball.

'That's where I left it! In the beach hut!'

She threw her racket down in the courtyard, dropped the ball, and ran. It had suddenly come back to her, quite vividly. The day after the dance – that last swim in the sea, the last of the year! She'd taken her watch with her and – of course – she must have left it in the beach hut. It would still be there. Better run, it would soon be getting dark. It got dark by tea-time at this time of the year.

She got to the beach as dusk was falling. How different Trebizon Bay looked in winter! From the top of the sand dunes she could see the big, empty expanse of it. The sea looked wild and rough, grey waves and white foam, breaking on to a lonely shoreline. In the distance the beach huts stood in a forlorn little row, the gulls crying about them.

Rebecca ran down the dunes and sprinted across the sand.

Breathing fast she reached the row of beach huts. She and Tish had shared the big one at the end! She got to the door and tugged it open. The hinges made a horrible creaking sound.

It was dark inside . . .

A sinister looking figure rose from the floor.

Rebecca screamed.

He wore faded trousers, black jumper and a pair of dark glasses. His chin was stubbly and dark and unshaven. She screamed again as he grabbed her and placed his hand across her mouth, dragging her into the hut.

'Sssssh!' He let go of her. 'Quick, shut the door!'

She stared at him and now she recognized him.

'Robbie!' she said, aghast.

He looked panic stricken.

'What are you doing here?' he asked.

10
Looking after Robbie

'What am *I* doing here?' said Rebecca. She was angry about the fright she'd been given. 'What are *you* doing here, more like it?' Then, her eyes getting used to the semi-darkness, she saw that Robbie's face was haggard and drawn. He looked as though he hadn't slept much, or eaten much, for days. 'Oh, Robbie, are you all right?'

'Sorry if I scared you.' He took hold of her arm, more gently this time. 'Did you know I was here – has somebody seen me –?'

Rebecca shook her head.

'I came to find my watch –'

Robbie expelled his breath.

'Oh, it's *your* watch? It's over on the ledge there! That's all you came for?' He looked profoundly relieved. He let go of her arm. 'Don't you dare tell anybody I'm here, Rebecca!'

She stared around the little hut. Robbie's trunk was open, dirty clothes spilling out of it. The unwashed socks were especially smelly. On the floor was a pile of bracken and dried up seaweed, a bed of sorts. Robbie had been sitting there when she'd arrived. Fish and chip papers were screwed up in a corner of the hut. What a mess! There was a bottle of drinking water. The truth dawned upon her.

'You're living here!' she gasped. 'You didn't catch a train at all. You've been living here since last Sunday! But how –'

'I tricked the Head's chauffeur into driving me to the *bus* station, just round the other side of the headland, Easy.'

'Robbie!' Rebecca's lower lip was trembling slightly. At last she could tell him! 'We rushed down to the station on Sunday, to see you before you caught the train –'

'I couldn't get on that train!' Robbie cut in. His eyes were smouldering. 'I know I behaved stupidly. Lost my temper and smashed a window. Got myself chucked out of College for the rest of term. I accept that. I've no complaints. But there's one thing I can't accept!' he said vehemently. 'Virginia's convinced I did it! *I'm not leaving until I've found out who really did take the car and then I'll turn 'em in at Trebizon police station!* That'll show

94

her. After that,' he shrugged, 'I'll go home like a lamb.'

He fell into a brooding silence, staring into space. It was a silence that Rebecca didn't dare to disturb. In any case, she felt deflated.

Robbie was still crazy about Virginia, then! He was still carrying the torch for her and it burned with undiminished brightness.

'Sorry!' he said suddenly, coming out of his reverie. 'You were saying something and I butted in. That you all went down to the station –?'

'Yes, the six of us,' said Rebecca, in a flat voice. 'To tell you we all support you, even Tish. You'd phoned me – remember?'

'Great!' His face, tired and haggard though it was, suddenly lit up with a big, warm, Anderson-type smile. Rebecca's spirits at once improved. 'And you've questioned everybody, like I asked?'

'We've done more than that!' Rebecca said. 'We've searched outside Court House for clues and been up the Clifford Road. We've found the tree that the car hit – and we've even been to Bond's barn and searched that, too –' Her voice faltered. 'We've drawn a blank so far, though.'

'Never mind!' He had cheered up and he looked grateful. 'You've been doing your best. No clues at all?'

'Well,' Rebecca said dubiously. 'Tish thinks we've got a possible suspect. A girl in the Fourth Year called Margaret Exton –'

She explained all about it. When she'd finished, Robbie shook his head and laughed. 'Ridiculous! Typical Tish! No, it's not her. I think I *know* who the thieves are –'

'You do?' gasped Rebecca. '*Who?*'

Robbie was sitting on the edge of his trunk, frowning and intense, flipping the dark glasses on to his open palm.

'Some of the Pop Inn boys. The trouble is, proving it.'

The Pop Inn was a cheap café at the top end of the town

where a gang of local boys congregated. They were a tough lot and were sometimes in trouble with the police.

'You sure about that, Robbie?'

'I've been up there every night, drinking tea, watching them,' said Robbie. 'What d'you think of my disguise, by the way?' He put the dark glasses back on. 'They all wear these things, even though it's the middle of winter and half of them never seem to bother to shave.'

Rebecca glanced at him and shuddered, remembering the fright he'd given her.

'You'll pass,' she said.

'There's three of them I've got my eye on,' Robbie said. He was secretly rather pleased with himself. 'They boast amongst themselves about various cars they went joy-riding in, back in the summer, especially foreign ones or interesting ones. Last night I followed them all round the town and I saw them try the door of an Alfa Romeo.'

He took the dark glasses off and Rebecca could see that there was an eager light in his eyes.

'But Saturday's their big night! I've got to hang on somehow –'

'Saturday?' asked Rebecca.

'That's when they did Slade's car, remember? A Saturday night! The town's full of flash cars then. The boys go drinking and then likely as not they pinch a car. Only I'm going to be right there. I'll catch them at it red-handed and call the police and –'

'But they'd beat you up first, Robbie!' Rebecca said in horror.

He seemed to get angry.

'Look, Rebecca. You get back to school now. Forget it.'

'You must let me tell the others!' Rebecca pleaded. The look in his eyes scared her! 'Well – just Tish.'

'*Don't be daft!*' He gripped her shoulders. 'You'll tell nobody – anything – promise?'

'Okay, I – I promise,' sighed Rebecca.

He relaxed his grip. She stared at his haggard face and then looked round the hut. She was worried about him! She couldn't just leave him –

'Robbie, what did you mean about hanging on *somehow*? Are you eating? Have you got any money –?'

'Not much,' he admitted. 'The College gave me a train ticket and three quid for the journey the other end. I just go to the chip shop at night, the rest goes on cups of tea at the Pop Inn.'

'You don't eat all day?' asked Rebecca.

'So what!' snapped Robbie. 'Come on, Rebeck, you'd better get going. What time's your tea?'

She looked at his watch and then set her own.

'Quite soon,' she said. 'I'll go in a minute, but I'm coming back.'

'What for? It's risky –'

'I don't care!' said Rebecca. 'I won't let anybody see me. I'll bring you food and money. You can't go on like this.'

Food! Money! He gazed at her. He couldn't hide his gratitude.

'Guess who's not going to argue!' he said. Then he stared. 'Now what are you doing?'

Rebecca was collecting all the dirty clothes together and bundling them up inside a dirty shirt.

'I'll wash all this stuff for you – don't worry, I won't let anybody see it – it's squalid in here!'

She kicked the door open, looked round outside to make sure that the beach was still deserted and then – as the darkness gathered around her – sprinted off across the sand with Robbie Anderson's dirty washing bundled in her arms.

When she reached Court House, the coast was clear. Everyone had gone to tea. She raced into the laundry room and flung the clothes into the washing machine, shook in some soap powder, then switched it on.

She ran all the way to the main school buildings and was late for tea.

'Where *have* you been?' asked Tish.

'Practising for Saturday, yes?' said Mara.

It was horrible having to keep a secret from them – and what a secret! – and not being able to look Tish in the eye.

'I'm starving,' she said, taking three slices of bread and butter at once.

'You must be!' commented Sue.

Nobody saw Rebecca fold the thin slices of buttered bread and stuff them in her pocket. After a decent interval she reached for some more. Talk at the table had resumed, babbling all around her.

'... and then Miss Heath wrote in the margin ...' came Tish's voice.

There were shrieks of laughter.

Rebecca was thinking: *I've put it on the quick wash cycle, that takes about thirty minutes, so does tea. If I'm first out of the dining hall and run all the way, I'll get back to Court before anyone else. I've got to get the stuff out of the machine before anybody sees it!*

'Don't you remember, Beck?' came Tish's voice. She nudged her sharply in the ribs. 'Oi! Wake up!'

'Remember what?'

'The time you wrote that English essay and Miss Heath wrote in red in the margin DON'T ABBREVIATE!'

Everyone laughed again and Rebecca managed to raise a smile.

'Where are you dashing off to?' asked Sue, as soon as tea finished.

'My – my racket!' said Rebecca, with sudden inspiration. 'Left it out in the courtyard – looks like rain. See you later!' And she was gone.

It was true enough – about the racket. Rebecca took the track that led to Norris House, scooped up her tennis racket and ball from the courtyard where she'd flung them down earlier, then hurried across towards Court House.

'I left the light on in the laundry room!' she thought, looking along the row of windows at the back of the boarding house. 'Unless someone's in there.'

She let herself in by the kitchen door, rushed along to the laundry room and burst in. Then she stopped dead. There was somebody bending down in front of the washing machine, about to open the porthole door!

It was Mrs Barrington!

'Oh, hallo, Rebecca,' said the housemistress, turning round. 'Is this your washing? The machine's just stopped. I was going to take it out and put these towels in ...'

'I'll do it!' choked Rebecca, grabbing a plastic basket and coming up to the machine with such momentum that Mrs Barrington had to step hurriedly aside.

Rebecca bent very close to the porthole door to shield what lay within and gingerly opened it. As she hauled the garments out and dropped them into the basket, she screwed them up as tightly as she could, so that they'd be unrecognizable. Shirts ... socks ... a jumper ... underpants! She could feel Mrs Barrington's presence, right behind her. She worked as fast as she could and her face was burning.

'All right?' asked the housemistress pleasantly, as Rebecca moved away with her basket, one arm over the top of it. Mrs Barrington moved forward with her load and bent down to put the first towel in. 'Oh, Rebecca –'

'Yes?'

Rebecca was tipping Robbie's clothes into the tumble dryer as fast as she could go, over in the corner of the room. Now she turned, a horrible feeling in her stomach, as Mrs Barrington advanced upon her, holding aloft one of Robbie's navy blue socks.

'You've left this in the machine,' she said. 'One of your hockey socks by the look of it.'

'Thanks!' Rebecca almost snatched the sock from her and flung it in with the rest. She switched on the tumble dryer and leant against it, protectively, feeling almost faint with relief.

'There,' said Mrs Barrington, a minute later, as she straightened up and switched on the washing machine. 'Going to be in here long?'

'Yes!' said Rebecca quickly. The tumble dryer was an old model and would take about thirty minutes to get Robbie's clothes bone dry.

'Be an angel and put the towels in the dryer for me when they're done?' said Mrs Barrington. Rebecca nodded. 'Good girl!'

So when her five friends came looking for her, a few minutes later, Rebecca was able to say quite truthfully:

'Can't come. I'm drying some of our towels for Mrs B.'

'We're wondering how to find out if Margaret Exton's got a boy friend,' said Tish. 'We're going to have an Action Committee meeting.'

'Tish still thinks Margaret took the car!' said Sue, catching Rebecca's eye.

'And she could be right!' Mara said loyally.

'Come on, Rebeck!' said Tish impatiently. 'Let's all go and make some coffee. We need your great brain and your photographic memory on this. Maggie Exton must know *some* boys. Who might have come with her in the car that night? Come on – you can leave that stuff drying.'

Rebecca was leaning against the dryer, hands on the lid. She felt edgy.

'It's a waste of time!' she said. 'I think you're barking up the wrong tree.'

'Drop it, Tish,' said Sue. 'Rebecca's just as worried about Robbie as the rest of us but she's got Saturday to think about. She's missed a lot of practice this week over this.'

'True,' said Tish. She looked at Rebecca guiltily now. 'I don't blame you for being a bit fed up with it all. See you later.'

Rebecca's lip trembled as they all trooped out. If only they knew! She longed to run after them and tell them where Robbie was, and how pleased he was that they were trying to help him. Most of all she wanted to tell them what he was planning to do on Saturday night, and how scared she was for him.

But she couldn't, of course.

Instead she crept down to the beach just before nine o'clock, with her small torch to light the way. She carried a big plastic carrier bag. Inside were Robbie's clothes, clean and neatly folded, some food to keep him going – and money. It wasn't much, but it was all Rebecca had.

'I'll just leave the bag in the hut,' thought Rebecca. 'I expect he's gone into the town now.'

Then the moon came out and she saw him standing down by the shore, listening to the breakers, hands in his pockets. A lonely, distant silhouette, waiting for her to come back.

It wasn't safe to shout, so she whistled.

He ran all the way to meet her.

'Rebeck!' He took the bag from her and looked inside. 'You wonderful girl!'

Suddenly he dropped the bag and lifted her right up to his shoulders as though she weighed no more than a feather.

'Come on, I'll give you a lift back!'

They both laughed as he ran with her all the way across the sands, up over the top of the dunes and right up to the little wicket gate that led back into the school grounds.

Gently, he lifted her down.

' 'Night, 'night!' he said. 'Off you go! You haven't told anybody?'

'Nobody!'

She ran all the way back to Court House, thinking how strong Robbie was. If he did get into a fight on Saturday, maybe he'd come out of it all right.

Every spare minute on Friday, Rebecca practised her tennis. The Exonford Junior Indoor tournament was only one day away.

As soon as it got dark, she went down to the beach hut again and took Robbie a blanket and some more food. She'd cadged some cold sausages from the kitchen and heated up some tinned soup and put it in a vacuum flask.

She waited in the hut, so that she could take the flask back. Two candles cast a dim light and Robbie had blacked out the window. While he ate his supper with relish, Rebecca tidied up the hut a little bit for him.

'Going into the town?' she asked.

'Not tonight,' he replied. 'Mmmm. This soup *is* good. I went last night, after I saw you. I'm glad I did. I've found out all I need to know. Which pub they're meeting in tomorrow night. I'll be there!'

He leant forward and touched Rebecca's arm.

'That money you've loaned me makes all the difference. It means I can spend the evening in the pub and stick right close to them.'

'Robbie –' began Rebecca.

She was about to say that he was under-age to go in pubs and that if he were caught he'd probably be expelled from Garth for good. But she knew it would be a waste of breath.

'Don't worry,' he said. 'I'll only be drinking shandy. But tomorrow's the big day!'

Once again she felt frightened for him.

She didn't even tell Robbie that tomorrow was her big day, too.

11

Rebecca *v.* Madeleine

'Tish!' whispered Rebecca tensely. It was in the middle of the night and she was kneeling by Tish's bed, gently shaking her. 'Wake up a minute. I want to talk to you.'

Rebecca couldn't sleep. She'd tossed and turned for

hours, listening to Tish and Sue's peaceful breathing in the other beds until she could have screamed out loud.

She'd said the words a hundred times in her head –

Tish – we've got to do something!

'You awake, Tish?'

'Uh?' The head of dark curls moved on the pillow and the eyes flickered open. 'Whassamatter?'

'Tish, I can't sleep. I'm worried about Robbie –'

'Oh, him. Aren't we all?' She reached up her arms and gave Rebecca an affectionate hug. 'Don't be. Go back to bed. You've got to play tomorrow – remember?'

'I –'

The words wouldn't come. Rebecca suddenly felt ashamed of herself. What on earth could Tish do about it? She couldn't tell Robbie what to do, any more than Rebecca could. She'd just be worried stiff, that's all.

The tension was broken. Rebecca went back to bed and at last fell asleep.

When the rising gong went she was achingly tired, but she felt better after she'd washed and had breakfast. It was Saturday, November 28th – tournament day! If she did well, and especially if she beat Madeleine Marks, she'd be promoted into the D squad in the new year. If she didn't ...

'Good luck,' said Joss Vining, outside the dining hall. 'They'll have the selection meeting tonight, after the tournie. They'll phone Miss Willis tomorrow if you've been picked. So you'll soon be put out of your misery. I'd love to see you get a place, Rebecca!'

The six walked back to Court House together. Rebecca went to get ready.

'She looks tired,' said Sue anxiously. 'Have you ever seen her so tense as she's been the last couple of days?'

'She's in a hurry to do well!' said Tish. 'She should have been pushed into the game when she was about nine, but she didn't have that kind of chance. Now she wants to make up for lost time. She doesn't want any setbacks. But she's worried about that stupid brother of mine, too ...'

Tish frowned, remembering.

They all flocked round Rebecca when she was ready to leave, the three A's, Elizabeth, Jane and Jenny as well, patting her on the back. 'Good luck!' Even some Fourth and Fifth Years joined in. Then, at the front door of Court House, Virginia Slade came up to her.

'Lots of luck,' she said. 'I know David thinks you're pretty good.'

Virginia was so sweet-tempered normally that Rebecca was surprised at the sharp little note in her voice when she spoke the name *David*.

'By the way,' she added, 'give him my love when you see him.'

She walked away. Rebecca watched her go, puzzled. But Mara, who was just beside her, gave her a nudge.

'Poor Virginia. I think she has been dropped, yes?'

'I wonder?' said Rebecca. She remembered how, in the weeks before the Hallowe'en Dance, Virginia was always dashing off on her bicycle to meet someone, eyes sparkling, prettily dressed. But she hadn't really noticed her doing that since. Not since the dance. 'You could be right, Mara.'

'The French call it La Ronde!' shrugged Mara. 'The round!'

'The round? What on earth are you talking about?'

'Robbie likes Virginia ... but Virginia likes David ... but David like you ...'

'Oh, Mara! Don't be silly. Shut up!'

'... and you like Robbie!' finished Mara. 'You see, you have to. That completes the circle!'

To Rebecca's utmost relief Mrs Barrington appeared with the car and honked the horn and wound down the car window.

'Come on, jump in, Rebecca. We don't want you to miss that train!'

'Just get on the courts and play to win,' said David Driscoll. He was giving them all a pep-talk in a quiet corner of the Exonford sports centre. 'The tournament, as you know, is singles only. Divided into two sections – boys and girls. It's raining so we're confined to the indoor courts. We've got to keep everything moving smartly all day. Finals at seven o'clock this evening.'

His hair was neatly combed and parted as usual and he wore the red county track suit, with various badges on the jacket.

'I expect you all to get through the first two rounds easily enough. You'll be mainly up against kids who only play in the summer – keen, though, most of them! Mrs Seabrooks wants to take a look at them while she's here today. But it's when we get to the semi-finals and the finals that it should be interesting.' He seemed to be looking at Rebecca and smiling at her. 'Right, go and get some coffee all of you. First three matches ten minutes from now.'

He drew Rebecca aside for a moment.

'You look tired. Something on your mind?'

Rebecca shook her head.

'Okay. Remember everything I've told you. About getting pitched up to win. Fight for every point. Concentrate.'

Wanting to win came naturally to Rebecca. When they broke for lunch she was safely through her first two rounds and into the girls' semi-final. So was Madeleine Marks, in the other half of the draw. Victoria had fallen to a girl from the local high school and she looked woebegone.

'I'll be out of the reserve squad now. That girl Catherine will come in in January. Just see if she doesn't.'

Mrs Seabrook, the county tennis scout, came over to say good-bye.

'I've got to go now. It's all meetings today! Good luck, those of you still left in. I'll hear all about it tonight!'

So Joss was right, thought Rebecca. A selection meeting took place tonight, straight after the tournament! They'd sort out the sheep from the goats.

Rebecca had to wait a long time for her semi-final match. With only the indoor courts in use, there was a backlog of matches to get through – mainly the boys' second rounds – and some of them were long and hard-fought. But at four o'clock a court became free for the first semi-final. It was Rebecca versus Catherine, the girl who'd given Victoria such a trouncing. She was only eleven but already a formidable little player.

'She's not going to beat me though,' Rebecca decided.

Rebecca took the first set 6–3. In the second set Catherine fought like a tigress to level 4–4 and that goaded Rebecca into devastating form. She raced for every shot, no matter how impossible it looked, and got everything back – then retaliated with some beautiful passing shots and winning volleys. She won the second set 6–4 and with it the match.

She was through to the final!

'Doesn't she move beautifully?' David Driscoll commented to Miss Davenport, the middle-aged lady coach who would be taking over the reserve squad after Christmas. 'Don't you think she's a find?'

'A natural. Very fast – and very, very graceful. There's a girl who should have started really young! She's not in command of all her strokes yet ...'

Rebecca walked past them, in a blur, and went to the cafeteria. All day she'd been fighting off her tiredness with sheer will-power – she must go and sit down now, get some tea. She mustn't give in!

Sometime later Madeleine Marks came in, full of bounce and vigour. She'd won her semi-final. Just as David and his colleagues had planned it, when they'd made up the draw, the final was going to be Rebecca *v.* Madeleine.

She was aching now. She was so tired! She was down
1–3 to Madeleine in the first set. Madeleine was such a
solid, chunky player ... thwack, wallop, thwack ... playing from the baseline, getting everything back. Try a tiny
drop volley, just over the net, make her run ... she can't
move very fast ... done it!

Concentrate! Fight back! Tell yourself you're not tired
... that's it ... your game's beginning to flow now – a
winning smash, straight down the line. 2–3, your service.
Serve to the line, right on her backhand, well done! A
feeble return, looping up – race to the net – punch the
volley home! Level 3–3. Madeleine to serve.

It's late now. It's dark. Saturday evening. What's
Robbie doing? He'll have left the beach hut now. He'll
be out in the town ... *what's happened? You've lost the
game!* Concentrate. Change ends. *Don't look at the clock.*
Half-past seven. He'll be in some pub or other, watching
those boys. Watching and waiting ...

Concentrate! You've got to serve. You're 3–4 down and
if you lose this game it'll be 3–5 and Madeleine to serve.

Robbie's wrong! The more you think about it ...
What's he doing trailing those boys around? They never
took the car ... *Fault!* It's obvious! *Love-fifteen.* They'd
never have bothered to hide it in the barn ... just dumped
it and run for it ... what sort of person WOULD bother?
– that's the mystery ... *Love-thirty.* Whatever they get up
to tonight, it won't prove a thing ... *Love-forty* ... concentrate, you've got to *concentrate!* ... oh, Robbie. You
don't stand a chance ... and it's all for nothing, anyway.
Game to Miss Marks. Miss Marks leads by 5 games to 3.

Madeleine won the first set 6–3 and the second 6–0.

They were shaking hands at the net.

It was all over. The match had slipped away from
Rebecca, just like that.

Her chance had slipped away, too. It must have done. No D squad after Christmas now. She felt like death.

Rebecca got her things and made a quick exit from the Exonford sports centre.

The big modern building with its flags flying was set a hundred yards back from the road. She had to cross a wide expanse of paved forecourt as big as a football field, lit by orange fluorescent lights. Then she'd be safely swallowed up in the anonymity of Station Road, which lay beyond a line of trees.

She ran and she didn't look back. She was nervous that somebody might see her, call her back. She felt utterly miserable. She didn't want to talk to *anybody*! She just wanted to get away fast, to the station, on to a train!

The puddles on the forecourt gleamed orange. Her tennis shoes padded as she hurried along. Everything was silent. Nobody called.

Then she heard a strange sound, somewhere behind her. *Squeak ... whirrr ... squeak. Squeak ... whirrr ... squeak.*

The noise sent a shiver down her spine.

She'd heard it somewhere before! When? Where?

She refused to look back, but the sound was getting louder, closer.

'Rebecca!' came a hissing whisper.

She'd reached the trees. Slowly, she turned round.

David Driscoll was chasing after her on his moped. But he, too, didn't want to be noticed. He was doing a strange thing. He was pedalling the heavy moped with the engine switched off.

The *squeak* was the sound of the pedals as they drove the thick chain round without engine power and made it *whirrr* like the fluttering of a bird.

Squeak ... whirrr ... squeak. Rebecca stared at the pedals going round. She was fascinated by the sound, but she didn't know why.

'Don't run away!' He caught her up and dismounted. 'You silly little goose.'

'I lost,' said Rebecca miserably.

'I'm still going to recommend you ... Come out of the light, we're in full view.'

'Recommend me?' gasped Rebecca, as he took her arm and they stood under the tree together. The leaves were dripping rain down on her blonde head.

'Of course!' said David. 'I don't know what's on your mind today, you completely lost concentration in that final. But so what! I'm going to get you into the D squad, even if it means a fight. The meeting's in less than half an hour.'

'But – but – why?' Rebecca felt faint with relief.

'Because you're the best, that's why!' He gripped her arm tightly and looked very intense. 'I'll be leaving for London after Christmas. And I'll go knowing that I've put you on the right road. That makes me feel good, Rebecca, because I think you're going to be great one day.'

Rebecca was silent. She was overwhelmed.

'I like you. We're the same type,' he said. He didn't seem to want to let go of her arm and suddenly she began to feel uncomfortable. 'Neither of us has been born with a silver spoon in our mouths. We're going to fight our way to the top! We'll meet up again – you'll see. One day, when you're a famous tennis player and I'm a big tycoon ...' He laughed in elation. 'I'll take you out! In my Alfa Romeo. Or would you prefer to go in my Ferrari? But that's all in the future –' He dropped her arm. 'I've got to go.'

He walked over to his moped and gave it a little kick, as though in disgust. Rebecca felt uneasy. Those were fast cars he'd been talking about – sports cars! He'd always given the appearance of not being interested in such things. But he was!

She could suddenly sense it. He hated that moped! Beneath the restrained exterior was another David Driscoll just roaring to get out.

Squeak ... whirrr ... squeak. Now she knew where she'd heard that eerie sound before! At the back of Court House, at three in the morning, the night John Slade's car went missing!

What was he doing collecting his moped at three in the morning and riding it away with the engine switched off? Because *that* was the sound she'd heard. What had he been doing between midnight, when he left Virginia, and 3 a.m. ... ?

'Training next week. Last session,' David was saying. He was about to wheel his moped back to the sports centre. 'See you then, Rebecca.'

The barn! The heart of the mystery. Those hay bales were heavy. But who stronger than David?

How might it all have happened that night? Was he feeling elated? A job at last ... a brand new driving licence ... Virginia Slade crazy about him! And there was her father's car sitting there ...

Was that it? A moment's madness ...

Then – disaster! What to do? Revert to type. Keep calm. The car's damaged! Tidy it away ... neatly, carefully. Somewhere nobody's going to find it for months. Then – any little clue, you could never be sure, any questions to be asked – he'd be gone!

'David?'

'What?'

'Why *those* cars?' she asked him. Her mouth felt dry. 'Why not a Masters X 19?'

12
The Ultimatum

'So you know?' He looked suddenly ill. His pallor was enhanced by the weird orange lighting of the place. He let his moped drop to the ground.

'I've known from the beginning it wasn't Robbie Anderson,' said Rebecca. 'Now I know it was you.' She was beginning to feel angry. 'You came back to get your moped that night. It was in our courtyard. It was three o'clock exactly. Don't you remember seeing my light?'

'Yes.' David Driscoll vividly remembered a light coming on in one of the ground floor rooms of Court House, just as he was creeping over to get his moped. It had worried him all along. 'So it was you? You switched it on – and then off again. You were watching me then!'

He drew her back into the shadow of the trees. He seemed relieved. 'You've known all along and you've shielded me!'

'Wrong!' snapped Rebecca. 'It's only just dawned on me.'

'What –' His voice was carefully modulated, everything under control. 'What, if anything, do you intend to do about it?'

Rebecca thought she knew exactly what she intended to do.

'Telephone Mr Slade – right now!' she replied. *He'll send a party into the town and find Robbie. Before it's too late*, she thought. 'That's what!'

'You can't prove anything!' He was getting rattled. 'I'll tell them you're a little liar –'

'Don't be daft,' said Rebecca. 'The police took finger-prints.'

He started shaking her, hissing.

'You can't do this to me, you can't. You'll ruin me! I've got to have a clean driving licence for this job – this would *ruin* me, Rebecca –'

'What about Robbie?' she hissed back. She was boiling with anger. 'You let him take the blame! He's in all sorts of trouble already and tonight he's going to get involved with some really nasty characters, if I can't find somebody to stop him, because he thinks they took the car –'

David Driscoll wasn't even listening.

'Robbie Anderson!' he said contemptuously. He let go of her and became icily calm, as though he'd received a douche of cold water. It was now clear to him what had been on Rebecca's mind all day. 'Robbie Anderson will be all right. His sort always are. They'll take him back at Garth next term, I daresay. Even if they don't, *Daddy* will get him in somewhere else. You don't have to waste your time worrying about him!'

He was beginning to tremble a little.

'It's just an episode for him. It's my whole future. You're not going to give me away are you, Rebecca?' There was something rather threatening about his manner now. 'You'll shield me, won't you?'

She was silent.

'If you won't even do this for me,' he spoke the words very carefully, 'why on earth should I do anything for you? It's not going to be easy getting you into the county squad, after the rubbishy way you played that final. Mrs Seabrook thinks a lot of Madeleine Marks. She and Mrs Marks play bridge together.' He threw that bit in sneeringly. 'You see what we're up against, Rebecca? I'd really have to fight for you at this meeting tonight. Why should I? Why should I bother?'

It was an ultimatum.

Still Rebecca said nothing.

She'd realized it might come to this. It didn't shock her. What did shock her was that she should feel so tempted.

This job *did* mean everything to David Driscoll and it was quite true what he'd said. He hadn't been born with Robbie Anderson's advantages.

Getting a place in the county squad meant just as much to her. It was only now, faced with David's ultimatum, that she realized *just* how much it meant ... how much she wanted it. Her ambition had grown and hardened in the past few weeks. If only she'd had the chance to begin tennis earlier, like that girl Catherine! Or Josselyn Vining.

Now time was running out. Another year and it might be too late to make any kind of a name for herself in junior tennis. They were playing at Wimbledon at fourteen now!

Why not do as David asked, protect him?

'Well?' He saw her hesitation.

Rebecca was filled with shame, that she had paused, even for a moment.

'You creep!' she said. 'I don't *want* you to do anything for me.'

She turned and ran through the dripping trees and into Station Road, her feet scuffling through damp autumn leaves. Her eyes were fixed on the telephone box that stood half way up the hill to the station.

David Driscoll stepped out from between two trees and watched her hurry off along the wet, shiny pavements. He saw her slow down by the red telephone box. Stop. Go inside. Pick up the telephone.

He returned to his moped and lifted it off its side. Then he wheeled it, very slowly, back towards the sports centre. It was raining again now, plastering his hair down very flat.

Some of the county officials were arriving in their cars. It was almost time for the meeting to start.

'I'm very pleased you've telephoned me, Rebecca,' said Robbie's housemaster. He was badly shaken, but he was taking great pains to hide the fact. 'Dr Simpson's out this evening and if Driscoll's at a meeting, there's nothing we can do tonight. I'll contact this young man in the morning and ask him to come to the College, to talk to us. If it turns out that what you say is correct, it will then be a matter for the police.'

'It is correct, sir,' said Rebecca. 'But it's Robbie Anderson I'm worried about –'

'Don't be,' Mr Slade said. 'There's nothing to worry

about.' Rebecca's story had filled him with alarm, but he was putting a calm face on things. 'I'll organize a search party and bring him straight back to College – before he does anything reckless!' He was very reassuring. 'I'll probably go down to the town myself. Yes, I will. He won't have come to any harm yet, but I'm very pleased you've rung me. Just leave everything to us. Anderson will be all right.'

So that was that. Rebecca put the phone down. It was done. They'd find Robbie – he'd be all right now. She hurried to the station and just caught a train. She slumped in a corner of the carriage. Tears came to her eyes.

By now, the selection meeting would be taking place.

They were tears of fury and disappointment. *I wish I'd never met you, Robbie Anderson*, she thought. *I just wish I never had.*

David has the Last Word

But Robbie was nowhere to be found in the town.

'Daddy's frantic about him!' said Virginia Slade, burst-
ing in on the six friends at ten o'clock that evening. They
should have been in bed. They weren't! They were loll-

ing around in Rebecca's room, in their pyjamas, talking in whispers. Rebecca had told them everything – except why she wasn't going to get what she'd so badly wanted. 'He's on the phone now. He wants to know if he's shown up here this evening –'

'Of course he hasn't!' said Rebecca in alarm.

'Have they searched the town?' demanded Tish.

'He's nowhere in the town and they've been to the police station and –'

'And *what*?' said Rebecca.

'The police are wondering now. A boy phoned them about nine o'clock. He said he was in the box opposite the Hotel Metropole and some youths were breaking into a white Mercedes car there. Then the line went dead! They sent a patrol car down straight away but the white Mercedes was still there and everything was peaceful, so they just assumed it'd been a hoax . . .'

'That would have been Robbie!' said Mara, aghast.

'The toughs must have spotted him in the phone box and . . .' Tish felt sick and couldn't go on. Virginia was already rushing out of the room again, back to the phone.

'I'll tell Daddy he's not here! For heaven's sake go to bed, you lot. You shouldn't be up. There's nothing any of us can do. It's up to the police now!'

As soon as she'd gone, Rebecca put on wellington boots and threw her dark blue school cape on over her pyjamas. She raised the sash window and put one long leg over the sill.

'Where are you going?'

'The beach hut! If he's hurt, that's where he'd make for!'

'But why?' asked Tish. 'That would be crazy. Why not just wait for the police to arrive –'

'How does *he* know he's in the clear now? He's not supposed to be here! He thinks nobody knows! Don't forget the College sent him home a week ago and he didn't go and that's pretty serious ... quick, chuck me your torch, Sue!'

'Wait for us!' shouted Tish, but Rebecca was already sprinting off across the courtyard.

She ran all the way down to the beach in the darkness, torchlight bobbing ahead. There was a heavy swell on the sea after the day's rain and she could hear the waves thundering and crashing on to the shore, somewhere down there in the blackness.

Robbie wasn't in the beach hut.

Rebecca flashed the torch all round the beach, feeling more and more anxious.

Then suddenly, the beam caught something. A figure, slumped forward beside some rocks –

'Robbie!' She ran and came up behind him.

He was kneeling down by a rock pool, dousing his face over and over again in the cool, still water. He turned towards her –

'Rebecca!'

Shining her torch, she saw that his lip was swollen and his nose seemed to have been bleeding. He was hurt, not badly, but all the hope had drained out of him.

'Robbie!' She crouched beside him and put her arm and part of her cape round his shoulders. 'Look at you! Report them to the police!'

'How can I, Rebeck! It wasn't the three villains I've been watching all week – it was some other louts. I wouldn't even recognize them again. I've had it now! I've run out of money *and* time –'

'Robbie!' Rebecca tried to tell him.

'– Dad gets back tomorrow. In the morning I'll catch the first train and go home and face the music ...'

'Robbie, your housemaster knows you're here. He's frantic. He's been out looking for you –'

'Slade?' Robbie looked furious. 'How –'

'I phoned him and told him –'

'You *what*?'

'– because I've found out who really took his car! I don't think anybody cares about you breaking that window now. I don't think they're going to hold it against you. After the way David Driscoll's behaved –'

'David Driscoll?' said Robbie in disbelief. 'David *Driscoll*?'

There came a shriek of excitement from somewhere across the sand. A row of bobbing torches were coming this way.

'Robbie's here!' cried Tish. 'He's all right! Rebecca's found him!'

Margot and Elf raced back ahead of the others to see Mrs Barrington and warn her that Robbie had been found and was cold, tired, hungry and in need of first aid.

Virginia Slade heard the commotion and she was waiting outside Court House when they brought him up from the beach.

'Robbie!' she ran forward. 'Thank goodness! Oh, your poor face!' She gazed at him, then lowered her eyes hurriedly, overcome with shame. 'Robbie – you've no idea how awful I feel ... I was so *wrong* about you – so was Daddy. We all were. No wonder you got so mad!'

She reached out her arms and hugged him tight and buried her face in his shoulder.

'Sorry, Robbie. Sorry, sorry, sorry.'

Robbie Anderson looked unspeakably happy.

Tish looked at Rebecca and gave an ironic shrug of the shoulders.

Rebecca just turned away.

'I'm going to bed,' she told Tish. 'I'm dead tired. See you in the morning.'

Robbie caught up with her in the hall and took her arm.

'Rebeck, you've been marvellous. You've done so much.'

'It's all right, Robbie.' She *was* dead tired – achingly tired – she just wanted to crawl into bed and sleep for a thousand years. 'See you.'

If only he knew how much! she thought, as she passed on down the hall.

When Rebecca woke, quite late on Sunday morning, she was stiff from all the tennis. She also felt achingly miserable and for some reason started to cry the moment Tish and Sue mentioned Robbie's name. It was some kind of reaction setting in.

'What's wrong?'

Her two best friends came and sat on the bed.

'Tell us, Becky.'

She told them exactly what had taken place between her and David Driscoll.

'The rotten so-and-so!' said Sue, angrily.

'I hope he gets sent to prison!' exclaimed Tish, in a fury. 'As for Robbie, that boy's just born lucky to have someone like you ...'

There was a tap on the door.

Sara Willis, the games mistress, put her head into the room. She'd just washed her hair and it was full of bounce and she looked in one of her cheerful moods.

'Good news, Rebecca! Still in bed?'

'Uh?' said Rebecca, wiping her pyjama sleeve across her eyes.

'Mrs Seabrook's just phoned me! You're in!'

'In?' asked Rebecca stupidly. 'In what?'

But Tish and Sue were already whooping.

'The junior D. You've been promoted! You're going in a county squad in the new year!' said Miss Willis, smiling patiently. 'I don't have to tell you how pleased and proud I am.'

'It was decided last night –?' gasped Rebecca.

'That's right. It was a close decision between you and

Madeleine Marks. But apparently David backed you all the way. And David has the last word! He's been coaching the reserve squad, so he should know!' she added happily. 'Time to get up, Rebecca!'

She was gone.

'Well ...!' said Rebecca.

'Well, well!' said Sue.

'Well, well, *well*!' finished Tish.

When the six of them went off to Moffatt's to celebrate, and discuss the whole story, Mara alone refused to be surprised.

David Driscoll didn't go to prison. He didn't even get reported to the police. Virginia Slade was a little bit annoyed about that.

'Robbie actually *pleaded* for him!' she told Rebecca on the Sunday evening. She'd been having tea with her parents and had just got back. 'Dr Simpson had Daddy bring them both to his study this morning. Daddy was all for handing David over to the police but David told them some terrific hard luck story about how he'd lose this job he's going to! So then Dr Simpson asked Robbie what *he* thought and Robbie actually stuck up for him! So all that's going to happen is that he's got to pay for the damage when he starts earning. Did you ever hear anything so ridiculous! What do you think, Rebecca?'

'I just think Robbie's nice,' said Rebecca.

'Yes.' Virginia thought about it for a moment. 'He is, isn't he?'

At tennis training the following Saturday, Rebecca saw David Driscoll for the last time.

He was very brisk all afternoon. Everything was very formal between them, as though nothing had happened.

When it was time to go, Rebecca went to find him. He

was sorting out some tennis balls at the back of the practice court.

'Thanks for what you did,' she said. She felt very awkward. 'Good-bye, David.'

He couldn't bring himself to look at her. He just kept on sorting out the balls.

'Thank Robbie Anderson next time you see him,' he said. 'Just say thanks, from me. He'll understand.'

'Okay. Good-bye, then.'

'Good-bye, Rebecca.'

It was surprising how quickly things returned to normal. Rebecca enjoyed the last two weeks of term. She was coming out top of III Alpha in English and French. In maths, after a long session with Miss Hort one dinner hour, she'd at last mastered simultaneous equations.

Christmas was approaching and there was a festive atmosphere at Trebizon, with decorations going up in the dining hall, the Christmas play to look forward to and then the Christmas carol concert. Margot, Sue and Mara were all in the choir this year.

Lessons with those teachers who couldn't keep order – and there were regrettably few of them at Trebizon, to Tish's way of thinking – were rapidly becoming riotous. Mrs Leonard, the hapless biology mistress, found herself firmly fixed to the bench in the science lab one morning, when a girl clamped the trailing end of her cardigan to the bench while she was leaning back on it and lecturing them on invertebrates.

For the six friends, the episode of the missing car passed into legend and made for a whole new stock of private jokes. Tish got teased a lot about Margaret Exton – and Rebecca about the time she did Robbie's washing. There was something else that they all found amusing.

'To think we questioned every single girl in Court about

whether they'd heard anything peculiar, that night the car disappeared!' said Sue. 'And all the time *Rebecca* was the one who'd heard something peculiar and she never connected it!'

They wondered if there might be any mysteries to solve next term.

'I hope so!' said Mara, little knowing then what she was saying.

At the very mention of the next term, Rebecca felt a thrill of excitement. She'd written to her parents to tell them that she'd been selected for junior county tennis training and matches.

Her name had been read out in assembly, too!

'I used to think you wanted to be a writer!' Pippa said to her that day. She'd produced a beautiful issue of the Trebizon Journal that term and at long last Jenny Brook-Hayes had had something published in it. 'In fact I was hoping you might submit something to Helena King for the Journal next term. But it looks as though you'll be too busy playing tennis. Perhaps you'll become a famous tennis player one day, instead!'

Tennis certainly seemed to be Rebecca's greatest interest in life these days.

When the boys in Robbie's house decided to hold a Christmas party and invited the girls of Court House over, en bloc, Rebecca didn't want to go. She was going over to Norris for the evening, she said. She and Joss were going to watch some international tennis on TV.

'Are you *sure*, Becky?' said Tish, standing in the hall of Court House in her red party dress. 'Come on, change out of those jeans, it'll be fun!'

Rebecca hesitated.

At that moment Virginia Slade came down the stairs with Alison Hissup.

Virginia looked delicately pretty in a gold dress embossed with a butterfly design. She had washed her hair and her eyes were sparkling.

Rebecca became very definite.

'Quite sure, Tish. I'm not interested in boys ... I'll just stick to tennis. Haven't I said that all along?'

Fiction for Older Readers from Granada.

Cover Drive Roy Brown   85p ☐
Rod Kirby is a fine cricketer but events force him to choose between his own interests and his father who has fallen into crime.

Dear Enemy Jean Webster   95p ☐
Sallie McBride tells the story, in letters to her friends, of how she transforms the John Grier Orphanage into a happy, love-filled home for 107 children.

Welcome Home Jellybean Marlene Fanta Shyer   85p ☐
Twelve year old Neil tells the story, in racy, schoolboy language, of his family's struggle to win acceptance for his mentally handicapped sister.

The Fight of Neither Century Robin Chambers   85p ☐
Five short 'other world and other dimensional' stories with a science fiction flavour.

Very Far From Here Dennis Hamley   75p ☐
Set in an English village at the time of the First World War, this is the story of two boys who become increasingly caught up in the adult world of suspicion and xenophobia.

Landings Dennis Hamley   75p ☐
The story of the effect on two brothers, one a conscript in the army, the other a school boy glider enthusiast, of the ghostly 'presence' of their grandfather who was killed in the First World War.

The Exeter Blitz David Rees   75p ☐
During World War Two the city of Exeter was severely bombed in a short series of raids. For Colin Lockwood, the blitz meant excitement and awe—until he realised the peril his family was in.

A Summer To Die Lois Lowry   75p ☐
The poignant story of two teenage sisters, the elder and prettier of whom is dying from leukemia. The younger sister comes to terms with death and with life through her family's harrowing experience.

Find a Stranger, Say Goodbye Lois Lowry   95p ☐
The warm and touching story of an adopted teenager's search for her natural mother.

D981

All these books are available at your local bookshop or newsagent, and can be ordered direct from the publisher or from Dial-A-Book Service.

To order direct from the publisher just tick the titles you want and fill in the form below:

Name _____

Address _____

_____

Send to:
Granada Cash Sales
PO Box 11, Falmouth, Cornwall TR10 9EN

Please enclose remittance to the value of the cover price plus:

UK 45p for the first book, 20p for the second book plus 14p per copy for each additional book ordered to a maximum charge of £1.63.

BFPO and Eire 45p for the first book, 20p for the second book plus 14p per copy for the next 7 books, thereafter 8p per book.

Overseas 75p for the first book and 21p for each additional book.

To order from Dial-A-Book Service, 24 hours a day, 7 days a week:

Telephone 01 836 2641 – give name, address, credit card number and title required. The books will be sent to you by post.

DIAL·A·BOOK

Granada Publishing reserve the right to show new retail prices on covers, which may differ from those previously advertised in the text or elsewhere.